100

TOO MUCH MAGIC

BY BETSY AND SAMUEL STERMAN
ILLUSTRATED BY JUDY GLASSER

D1044192

HarperTrophy
A Division of HarperCollins*Publishers*

For John, Rob, Andy and Susie
and their own special magic

Too Much Magic
Text copyright © 1987 by Betsy and Samuel Sterman
Illustrations copyright © 1987 by Judy Glasser

Manufactured in the United Kingdom by HarperCollins Publishers Ltd.
For information address HarperCollins Children's Books, a division of
HarperCollins Publishers,
10 East 53rd Street, New York, NY 10022.

Library of Congress Cataloging-in-Publication Data
Sterman, Betsy.
  Too much magic.

  Summary: Two brothers have a grand time wishing for all sorts of
things with the help of a magic cube the younger brother finds in the
playground.
  [1. Science fiction.   2. Magic—Fiction.   3. Brothers—Fiction.]
I. Sterman, Samuel.   II. Glasser, Judy, ill.   III. Title.
PZ7.S83815To   1987   [Fic]   85-45861
ISBN 0-397-32186-4
ISBN 0-397-32187-2 (lib. bdg.)
ISBN 0-06-440404-8 (pbk.)

First Harper Trophy edition, 1994.

CONTENTS

ONE

If my kid brother weren't such a nonstop weirdo, I guess I'd have paid more attention to him when he said he could make wishes come true with magic.

Magic? Come on!

Still, he did make the broccoli disappear.

The whole thing started on what seemed like just an ordinary Saturday. Mom and Dad and Jeff and I were sitting around the table finishing supper and Jeff was complaining about the

1

broccoli. Then suddenly he went quiet, as if he were thinking hard about something.

Dad got up to answer the phone and Mom pushed her chair back too.

"Okay, crew," she said with a smile. "If I'm going to get my weaving ready for the crafts show I'd better get to it right now. Bill, it's your turn to clear the table."

"Sure," I said. "What's for dessert?"

"Brownies and ice cream, but later. I'll see you in about an hour. Finish that broccoli, Jeff."

"Yeah, yeah," Jeff said, but as soon as she left he slammed down his fork and made a face at the broccoli. Then he started fooling around with something shiny he pulled out of his pocket.

I piled up some plates and headed for the kitchen. "Hurry up, yuckface," I called over my shoulder.

"I hate this stuff," I heard him say. "I wish I had a hot dog instead."

I know you're not going to believe this, but when I came back to get another load of dishes, there sat Jeff, munching away on a hot dog! A big, sizzling, ball-park hot dog!

"Where'd you get that?" I demanded.

"Wished it," he mumbled as he wiped a smear of mustard off his chin with the back of his hand.

"Sure, sure," I said. "Come on, where'd it come from?"

He shrugged his shoulders and muttered something that sounded like "magic," but his mouth was so full I couldn't really be sure.

It was crazy. Here he was, chomping away on a hot dog that hadn't been there two minutes ago. And the broccoli? The broccoli was gone.

I put both my hands on the table and leaned toward him. "Listen," I said, "tell me how you got that hot dog."

He met my scowl with a grin. "Told ya," he said. "Magic!"

And off he ran. I could hear him race up the stairs and slam the door of his room shut.

I took off after him and got there just in time to hear the lock click.

"Hey!" I yelled. "What's going on?"

"Go away," he yelled back.

"Come on," I yelled again. "What's with you?"

"Leave me alone, will ya? *Go away!*"

I shrugged, and went away. There's no messing with Jeff when he gets stubborn, and I could tell that this was one of his stubborn times.

I'll ask him about it later, I told myself. He'll be down for dessert.

He wasn't, and that was strange. Jeff's not one to pass up brownies and ice cream.

Well, that was just the beginning of all the strange things that happened for a whole week afterward.

Like the broken window, for instance.

On Sunday, the day after the hot dog, Jeff stayed in his room all day. That was unusual, but it was okay with me, because Danny came over that afternoon to practice soccer plays in the backyard and we both agreed it was great that Jeff wasn't around to pester us.

Danny and I had booted the ball around for about half an hour when I slammed a really hard one. Crash! Right through a basement window in the house next door.

"Cripes, Dan!" I shouted. "Why'd you let it get by you?"

"Are you kidding? Pelé couldn't have stopped that one."

We ran over to look at the broken window.

"Guess we'll have to pay for a new one, huh?" Danny said.

"Yeah," I answered with a sigh, "but the Hansons are away for the weekend. We ought to get it fixed for them in case it rains before they come back." I shot another look at the big jagged hole in the glass and said, "Come on, let's go tell my dad."

Dad was great. He didn't get mad at all. He just put down the Sunday paper and said, "Okay, let's go measure it. Then we'll find a hardware store that's open on Sundays and buy some glass and putty."

Over at the Hansons' house Dad asked, "Which window is it? I don't see anything broken."

"That one," I said, pointing. "Right, Danny?"

"I guess so," Danny said slowly. "I mean, I thought it was that one, but . . ."

Dad gave us both a strange kind of look. "Come on, fellas," he said with a smile. "There are only two basement windows on this side of the house, and neither one of them is broken. Are you putting me on?"

I stared at the windows. They weren't broken, either of them.

"But I saw it, and I heard it break," I said. "Danny heard it too, didn't you, Dan?"

Danny nodded in a puzzled way. "Anybody a mile away could have heard it," he said.

The three of us walked all around the Hansons' house. Not a single window was broken. There wasn't even a broken flowerpot anywhere.

"Well," Dad said with another of those wry smiles, "I think you boys have your calendar mixed up. April Fools' Day was a month ago."

After Dad went back inside, Danny and I just stood there. Neither of us knew what to say.

"Am I nuts?" Danny finally said. "I *know* I heard a window smash."

"Me too," I said. "This one right here."

I squatted down next to the window and

touched the solid, unbroken glass. Then I saw
something that made me jump back.

Inside the Hansons' basement, on the floor
near the washing machine, was my soccer ball.

"Look!" I shouted, and I turned around to
grab Danny and pull him down to see it too.
But just as I did, I caught sight of Jeff leaning
out of his bedroom window with his elbows
propped on the sill and his chin propped on his

hands. He was laughing like crazy but not making a sound.

All of a sudden I didn't want Danny in on this anymore. When he said, "Look at what?" I answered quickly, "Nothing. Listen, I've got to go in now. See ya tomorrow at school, okay?"

"Sure, see ya." With a wave he ran down the driveway. I ran too, straight up to Jeff's room.

I banged on his locked door and shouted, "Hey!" I really had to shout because the noise coming out of there sounded as if there were a whole video arcade behind the door.

"Hey!" I shouted again. "Open up! I want to talk to you!"

He didn't open up, but the noise stopped.

"Talk to me about what?" he asked.

All of a sudden I felt stupid, but I went ahead with it anyway. "About my soccer ball," I said. "It's in Hansons' basement."

There was silence on the other side of the door. Then he said, "Look again, creepo. It's right in the backyard where you left it."

"No way!" I shouted back. "That's not where it is!"

8

"Wanna bet? Look in the yard, right under the maple tree."

I went bamming down the stairs and out into the yard.

And there it was! Like Jeff said, it was right under the maple tree.

I picked up the ball and walked slowly over to the Hansons' house. Once more I squatted down outside that window, the window I knew had been broken. I squinted my eyes and peered in.

There was no soccer ball in there, not in front of the washing machine or anywhere else, but there was something that I'd missed the first time. On the floor of the basement were small, jagged pieces of broken glass.

I didn't say any more to Jeff about the whole weird thing. For one thing, I didn't know what to say, and besides, Jeff kept pretty much to himself all that week. He'd come dashing in from school and not even look at the snacks Mom had set out for us, but go straight up to his room as fast as he could. He was always mumbling about having a lot of homework to do.

I couldn't figure out the strange noises that kept coming from his room. A couple of times I thought I heard a dog barking, and often there would be those video arcade sounds.

There were strange smells too, smells like fresh-baked doughnuts and pepperoni pizza, Jeff's favorite kind.

"What's going on?" I asked a couple of times, but he skittered away from my questions. I tried to figure a way to bust in on him, but he always kept the door locked.

Mom was so busy with her weaving project that week that she didn't pay much attention. One day she did say something to Jeff about going up to run the vacuum cleaner in his room, and he just about split his seams.

"No!" he shouted. "I've got a lot of stuff in there for a science project. It's homework, and it'll get all messed up if anyone goes near it. Please, Mom, I'll clean everything myself, honest I will. Please!"

Mom gave in, but later I heard her say to Dad, "I wonder if I ought to call Jeff's teacher. It doesn't seem right for an eight-year-old to have to spend so much time on schoolwork.

Why, he never seems to have time to play any-more."

I didn't say anything, but it seemed to me that Jeff was playing a lot. Sometimes, when I was doing my own homework or working on my model dinosaur skeleton, I'd hear noises coming from his room—the clacking of an electric train set, the car chase sounds of TV shows, the beeps and buzzes of space-war video games. It didn't make sense, because Jeff didn't have any of those things in his room. But he didn't have a pizza parlor either, and yet . . .

The week went by and then it was Friday. That was the day Jeff got the motorbike.

A real motorbike! Wow, was it something! The kind of super-expensive, jazzed-up, pow-erful thing Dad would never let Jeff or me have in a million years.

I saw it in the garage the minute I got home from soccer practice. A shiny orange and black and chrome 100cc trailbike, with the price tag still on it and the name JEFF painted on the gas tank in fancy Day-Glo letters.

Jeff was hopping on and off the seat, making

11

brrrmmmm brrrmmmm noises, pretending to be riding even though his feet could hardly touch the ground.

"Holy cow!" I shouted. "Where'd *that* come from!"

"*Brrrrrrrmmmmmm brrmm brrmm*, wished it!" Jeff shouted back. "Just a couple of minutes ago. *Brrrrrrmmmmmmmmmmm!*"

"Don't give me that wishing stuff," I hollered angrily. "Where'd you get the bike?"

"Told you, I wished for it and here it is!"

I didn't get any further than that, for just then Mom and Dad pulled into the driveway. Were they ever mad when they saw that bike, and Jeff on it! It was a pretty hairy scene, with Dad demanding to know whose bike it was and Jeff saying it was his and then Dad yanking Jeff off the bike and Mom insisting that Jeff say where it came from and me saying I didn't know anything about it and Jeff hollering it hadn't cost anything so why couldn't he keep it. Our dad's a good-natured guy and fair about most things, but this was too much for him. He got madder and madder and so did Jeff. Pretty soon Jeff was crying as well as screaming and then, all of a sudden, he gave up. He stopped thrashing around and begging to keep the bike.

He turned away from all of us, his face red and furious.

"Okay! Okay!" he yelled. He jammed his hands deep down in the pockets of his jeans and shouted, "I wish the darned thing would go away! No, would get taken away!"

"Listen, Jeff," Dad said, "that isn't the point at all. What I want to know is—"

"Say, folks . . ." interrupted a man's voice. We all turned around. There, in the doorway of the garage, stood a deliveryman. It was as if he'd come from out of nowhere, but there he was, holding a tool kit in one hand.

"This goes with the bike," he said. "Sorry it got left behind." He held the tool kit out to Jeff and smiled. "Like your new bike, sonny?"

Dad didn't give Jeff a chance to answer. "Where did this bike come from?" he demanded.

The man pulled a piece of paper out of his pocket. "From the Hike 'n' Bike Shop," he said. "Here's the delivery order right here, see?

One 100cc Trailmaster, black and orange, deliver to Seventy-eight Pinecliff."

"Ohhhhhhhh," Mom said on a long breath. "It's a mix-up. This is Seventy-eight Pine*brook*."

The man squinted at the paper. "My gosh," he said. "I'm sorry about that. Well now, sonny, don't be too disappointed. Awful sorry about the mistake."

And before any of us could say anything more, he wheeled the bike out of the garage and down the driveway, loaded it into a truck, and drove away.

Dad put his arm around Jeff and said, "All that fuss for nothing." He handed Jeff his handkerchief, but Jeff wiped his nose on the back of his hand anyway. "Just a silly mistake," Dad said, "and here we got ourselves all riled up over it."

Jeff didn't say anything. He just stood there, looking down, angrily thumping the toe of his sneaker on the concrete floor.

"It's okay, honey," Mom said. She gave him a quick kiss on top of his hair, then picked up her shopping bag. "Bill, stay with him while Dad and I get things ready for supper."

Stay with him? You couldn't have dragged me away from him with a 100cc Trailmaster! I could hardly wait till the kitchen door closed behind Mom and Dad.

"Funny about that name painted on the bike," I said. "How come a bike with your name on it gets delivered here by mistake?"

"Shut up," he muttered angrily. "There's lots of Jeffs."

"Who do we know on Pinecliff with that name?" I asked.

"Lay off, will ya?" Jeff shouted. He stomped off into the house, but I didn't follow him. I just stood there, trying to figure it all out. There was something that kept bugging me.

All of a sudden it hit me. A mix-up with the streets, like the deliveryman said? No way! Nobody lives on Pinecliff. Not a guy named Jeff or anybody else. A month ago all the houses in that part of town were torn down to make room for a bunch of apartment buildings!

Something really weird is going on here, I said to myself. And I'd better find out fast!

TWO

Early the next morning Danny called.

"Guess what movie's at the Strand today!" he said excitedly. "*Summer of the Space Monsters*—want to go?"

"Do I ever!" I shouted.

"Great! Meet Frank and me there at one-thirty. So long."

I could hear the loom clattering in Mom's workroom, so I poked my head around the doorway and said, "I'm going to the movies with Danny and Frank this afternoon. It's that space monster movie we've been waiting for."

"Fine," she said, "but first . . ."

"I know. First clean up my room."

I ran upstairs, threw a week's dirty clothes down the laundry chute, hauled a lot of stuff out from under my bed, and moved some dust around. There was plenty of time so I worked on my model dinosaur for a while. I was trying to hitch some leg bones together when Mom came in.

"Bill," she said, "it looks like you're going to have to take Jeff to the movies with you."

"Aw, Mom!" I groaned.

"I know, he can be a pest sometimes with you and your friends, but . . ."

"*Some*times? How about *all* the time!"

"I'm sorry, honey, but Dad has a meeting at the bank this afternoon and I'm scheduled to teach at the crafts shop, and there's no one who can come over to baby-sit today."

"So let him stay home alone," I said.

She shook her head. "He's only eight, and he's—well, you know how he is."

"I sure do," I said grumpily as I put a handful

of plastic bones back into the box. "Do I have to have him tagging along with me all the time?"

"No, but I'm afraid you do this time." Her voice was quiet, but I knew she meant it.

"Okay," I agreed with a sigh. She gave me a smile and a quick hug before she left my room.

A few minutes later I went down the hall and listened at Jeff's locked door. There were no sounds from inside.

Maybe he won't even want to go, I thought to myself. Maybe he's still so mad about the motorbike that he'll want to stay home and sulk, or do his homework, whatever it is. Cripes, that'll be worse, 'cause then I'll have to stay home, too, and baby-sit. Nuts!

"Hey, Jeff," I called as I knocked. "Open up."

"Get lost," he answered. "I'm busy."

"Too busy to go to the movies? Mom says I've got to take you with me. Want to go?"

"You betcha!"

"Then open the door. I'll help you clean up

19

your room." Smart me, I thought. Here's my chance to see what he's been doing in there all week.

There was silence. "Jeff?" I called after a while. "Let me in, okay?"

Finally he unlocked the door. "You don't have to help me," he said. "It's all done."

It was. His room was neat as could be—no clothes hanging off chairs, no toys and stuff lying around all over the place. And nothing that could have made any of the weird noises I'd been hearing all week.

"Where's your homework project?" I asked as I looked around.

"Oh, I . . . I put it away," he said. "Hey, what are we gonna see? There's twelve cartoons at the Century. Let's go there!"

I shook my head. "No, it's *Summer of the Space Monsters* at the Strand."

"Yuck," he said. "I hate monster movies."

"Listen, this is supposed to be a really good one, and Danny and Frank are going too. You want to go or not?"

"Sure, but—"

"Then quit pestering. If you don't like it you

20

don't have to look at the screen."

He quit pestering, and I thought that was the end of it.

It wasn't, not at all.

Mom dropped us off in front of the Strand, and pretty soon Danny and Frank got there too. They weren't happy either to have Jeff tagging along, but we bought our tickets and popcorn and went in.

Summer of the Space Monsters started off great. Frank and Danny and I had a super time yelling whenever the monsters did something scary like invading a summer camp, but Jeff wiggled around in his seat something awful. We sent him to the bathroom twice and gave him money for more popcorn, but it didn't do any good.

"I don't like this," he kept whining. "It's scary."

"No it isn't," I whispered. "It's all make-believe, just like your dumb cartoons. Look at that freaky old monster up there. Can't you see he's made of rubber?"

But Jeff wouldn't look. He kept twisting around in his seat and yammering about how scary it was.

21

Finally I couldn't take any more of his squirming and whining.

"Knock it off, will ya?" I said. "You can't always have everything your own way."

He gave me an odd kind of look. Then he jammed his hands into his pockets and sat up straight in his seat. Over the rattle of my bag of popcorn I heard him say, "Oh, yes I can!"

And then the weirdest thing happened. The screen went dark for a few seconds, and when it lit up again the monster movie was gone and in its place was Mr. Magoo driving a jeep over Niagara Falls!

You can imagine the uproar! Everybody in the whole theater started to stamp and hoot. It got so bad that the lights came on and the manager climbed up on the stage. He waved his hands to quiet things down.

"We're . . . we've had some . . . um . . . technical difficulties," he said nervously. "But we'll soon have everything under control, everything under control."

Boy, was he wrong. The technical difficulties got worse. It turned out to be the most out-of-control afternoon at the movies ever.

Summer of the Space Monsters came on again, but every time it got to a really good part, like when the slimy, toad-faced monster was sneaking up on the kids at the beach, the film would jerk and snap, and the next thing you knew there would be some dumb cartoon again.

A lot of older kids got up and left. I could hear them grumbling about getting their money back. But we stayed to the very end. Danny and Frank and Jeff were laughing their heads off.

Not me. I sat there trying to shove away an uneasy thought that just wouldn't let go.

In some way, some way that I didn't understand, Jeff was involved in what was happening.

There he was, right beside me, whooping with laughter and behaving as nutty as everyone else each time a cartoon broke in. He was only a little eight-year-old kid, but in some crazy way he was making it all happen. I just knew it.

It was hot in the theater, but I felt cold all over.

All the way home from the movie Jeff chattered away with Frank and Danny, laughing at the crazy things that had happened.

"Remember when the guy who owned the camp went into the cave to look for the monster and all of a sudden . . ."

"Yeah, it switched to Bambi looking for Thumper in the forest!"

"And how about the time when the toad-faced monster was running after that little kid and *pow!* It turned into some dumb cat running after Mighty Mouse!"

"*Everything* kept changing from scary to funny! Great!"

I didn't laugh with them. For me, what had happened wasn't funny at all. I was scared, and it wasn't about monsters. It was about Jeff.

When we got home Mom and Dad were in the kitchen drinking coffee.

"How was the movie?" Mom asked.

"Terrific!" Jeff said. "It was the best!"

"It was okay," I said. I steered Jeff out of the kitchen and up the stairs, yanked him into my room, and shut the door. I looked him straight in the face. "Now listen," I said firmly. "Something kooky is going on with you. Something's been going on all week. You tell me what it is, right now!"

He flopped down on my bed and looked up at me. "I did tell you," he said. "You just didn't listen."

"Tell me again."

"I told you about the hot dog and I told you about the motorbike. It's like I said, magic!"

"MAGIC?"

"Yes, magic! I can make my wishes happen. Anything I wish for I can get."

"Nobody can do that!" I yelled.

"Yeah? Watch!" He looked around my room for a second. "Watch your dumb dinosaur model. I wish Bill's dinosaur model would get itself finished."

The next thing I knew, pieces of my dinosaur skeleton were floating up out of the box and hitching themselves together. A bunch of rib bones rattled into place next to each other, and a whole section of tail bones clicked together. Bones from the unfinished spine joined each other with soft little clattering sounds. Last of all the head floated out of the box, swung around the whole body a couple of times, and fastened itself to the end of the neck with a loud snap.

All of a sudden my own bones stopped holding me up. I sat weakly down on the bed, staring from the model to Jeff and back again.

Jeff was grinning all over. "That was neat!" he said. "Now watch this!"

The whole room seemed to be swimming around me, but I watched.

And you know what I saw? I saw my dinosaur model walk around on top of the table! Soon it was hopping, skipping, twirling around, flipping its tail and stamping its feet and waggling its head from side to side.

"How do you like that?" Jeff cried.

"Make it stop," I croaked.

"Aw, okay. I wish Bill's dinosaur model would stop."

It stopped. It just stood there. One perfectly put together plastic brontosaurus that could dance.

Jeff leaned back on his elbows. "See?" he said with a smirk. "I can make anything I wish come true. Now do you believe me?"

THREE

I managed to crawl off the bed and over to the door to lock it so there'd be no chance of Mom or Dad busting in on us. Then I dropped down next to Jeff again.

"Tell me," I said. The voice didn't sound very much like mine. "Tell me all about it."

"It" turned out to be a small metal cube that he dug out of his pocket. "Everything started happening after I found this," he said. I stared as he held it up in front of me.

"What is it?"

"It's a wishing cube. All you have to do is touch it and wish for something and your wish comes true."

"That's nuts," I said weakly. "How can a thing like that have anything to do with . . . with what a guy wishes?"

He shrugged. "I don't know, but it does. I even fixed the Hansons' broken window with it!"

"You fixed the window? With a *wish*?" I stared at the strange little cube in his hand.

All of a sudden he pushed it out toward me. "Here," he said. "Make a wish!"

I was almost afraid to touch it, but he shoved it into my hand.

It was about the size of an ice cube, and it had a soft metallic gleam, not as bright as silver but almost. It felt cool against the palm of my hand —not cold, just nicely cool. I poked at it with one finger and turned it around and around. It looked the same all over. Perfectly smooth and precisely square, the same on all six sides.

As I was looking it over Jeff chattered away, not waiting for me to ask any questions.

"I found it in the playground at the corner,"

he said all in a rush. "Last Saturday when I was coming home from Bobby's house. Remember? The day we had broccoli for supper and I got the hot dog?"

How could I forget!

"I was late so I cut through the playground and I saw this shiny thing in some weeds. It looked interesting so I went over to pick it up. Isn't it neat? It really makes wishes come true!"

"How?" I asked. My voice came out like a croak again.

"I don't know," he said with a shrug. "Who cares? It works. It really does. It's magic."

Magic. That's okay for a little kid like Jeff, but I don't believe in magic. In the real world there isn't any such thing. Even magicians' magic is really only tricks. Still . . .

I swallowed, trying to get rid of the thickness in my throat.

"Go ahead," Jeff said impatiently. "Wish something."

I don't know why, but I couldn't. I was too confused, or maybe too scared, to make any wish at all.

"Here, let me show you." Jeff grabbed the

cube out of my hand and looked around. "I wish . . . uh, let's see, I wish for a pillow fight! Just with pillows!"

Suddenly the pillow flew off my bed. Another one appeared from nowhere, and they started hitting each other. *Thump! Thump* again! It was like the big pillow fights Jeff and I had once in a while, but this time we weren't in it at all. We were at the side watching, laughing as the pillows bumped and swung against each other.

"More pillows!" Jeff yelled. "I wish there were more pillows in the fight!"

And there they were, ten, then maybe twenty pillows, all thumping away at each other in the middle of the room. It was the wildest pillow fight in the world!

I laughed till my sides hurt. "Make them stop!" I finally gasped, and Jeff wished it over. The pillows disappeared, all except my own, which drifted back to my bed and settled itself in place without a wrinkle in it.

"You're right!" I cried. "Who cares how the cube works. Give it here!"

I grabbed the cube from Jeff and closed my

fist over its cool smoothness. Pictures of swimming pools and piles of money went spinning through my mind. I could have everything, ABSOLUTELY EVERYTHING I'd ever wanted! My own TV set. That fancy digital watch I'd seen in a store downtown. A sailboat, no, a cabin cruiser, no, why not both! Even a horse, a whole stable of horses! Wowie! This was going to be great!

I started wishing. And from then on that afternoon was Christmas and the Fourth of July and all the birthdays in the world all mixed in together. It was WONDERFUL!

I started with the TV set, a big one, with a complete videotape unit to go with it. One wish and, *ping!* There it was! The watch? No sooner had I wished for it than I felt it on my wrist. Sneakers, the most expensive kind, in every color and style, *pow!* There they were, thirty-seven pairs of them, all lined up neatly at the foot of the bed except for the bright purple ones that suddenly appeared on my feet.

"Hey, give it here!" Jeff grabbed the cube back and did some wishing of his own. "I wish I had a whole set of matchbox cars."

Zap! There they were! A pile of games, comic books (lots and lots of those), baseball cards! There they *all* were, everything bright and glossy and new.

"My turn!" I shouted. "Watch this!"

Hockey skates! Skis, ski boots, poles! An all-star tennis racket! A video game as big as a pinball machine, with buzzers and flashing lights! The room was filling up with stuff, but we kept wishing.

We wished out loud and we wished in whispers and we wished silently in our heads. We wished holding the cube tightly and we wished holding it between two fingers. We wished standing, sitting, with our eyes open, and with our eyes closed. As long as we were touching the cube, whatever we wished for appeared. Instantly!

Now I knew what had been going on behind Jeff's locked door all week.

Finally, after all our whooping and hollering and jumping around, we were out of breath. We flopped down on the floor in the middle of all that wonderful mess, both of us panting and grinning at the same time.

"Wow!" I said again. It was all I could think of to say, but it expressed everything.

But Jeff had had a week's head start on this wishing business, and he knew something else to do.

"I'm hungry," he said. "I wish I had a hamburger."

Poof! There it was, hot and juicy in its sesame seed bun.

"Me too!" I grabbed the cube and wished myself a burger and an order of french fries. *Pow!* There they were!

I leaned back against a four-foot-high double stack of comic books and chewed away. If I'd had any suspicions that this might turn out to be only a dream, those doubts were gone now. The fries were hot and crisp, just the way I like them, with salt that crunched between my teeth. I could taste the burger, feel the glob of mustard that dripped down my chin. And the chocolate shake I wished for felt cool and creamy as it slid down my throat.

It was all real.

"Tell me again," I said to Jeff. "How did you get this cube?"

"Found it," he mumbled with his mouth stuffed full of potato chips.

"Just plain found it? In a patch of weeds in the playground?"

"Yup."

"Did you notice if there were any more like it lying around?"

"Nope. I mean I was in a hurry to get home so I don't know for sure."

I ate the last of the french fries and wiped my hands on my jeans.

"But how did you find out it could do what it does?" I asked.

"Sort of by accident. You know Mrs. Brauner's poodle?"

"Honeybun? Sure."

"You know how she keeps him tied up in her yard all the time? Well, that day, when I came running past her house, he got loose. Soon as he saw me he took off straight after me."

"So what? He's just a friendly little puppy."

"I know, dummy. I'm not scared of him. But once he followed me for blocks and I had to carry him back all the way to Mrs. Brauner. Last Saturday I didn't have time, so I stopped

and I patted him and I guess I said something like, 'I wish you were tied up like you oughtta be, Honeybun.' And then, all of a sudden, he was!"

"Just like that?"

"Yup. One minute he was jumping all around me barking like crazy and the next minute he was tied up to the lilac bush."

"Yeah, but . . ."

"And that wasn't the only thing that happened. When I got home I saw my skateboard in the middle of our driveway and I said to myself, 'Gee, I wish that thing was put away.' And Bill, you should have seen it! It rolled right along the driveway into the garage, all by itself, without me pushing it or anything!"

"So you figured out it was the cube doing all that stuff?"

"Not then. I knew something weird was going on, but I didn't know it was the cube till I didn't get the mustard."

"What mustard?"

"Well, all through supper I kept wanting a hot dog and then I wished for one and got it, and I wasn't too surprised about that, but while you were in the kitchen I wished for some mustard and I *didn't* get it. Then I *was* surprised. So I tried to remember exactly how everything had been when I'd wished before. And I figured out that when I'd made the other wishes I'd been holding the cube, or at least touching it."

"So you touched the cube and wished again for the mustard," I said, "and it worked."

"Yeah," Jeff said with a grin. "And afterward, up in my room, I had two more hot dogs and a banana split!"

I looked at the cube on the floor between us. I looked straight at it and I said, "Cube, I wish I had a pickle."

Nothing happened.

Then I reached out one finger, just one finger, very carefully, and I touched the edge of the cube.

"I wish I had a pickle," I said again.

Zing! There it was!

"I told you," Jeff said. "You have to touch it."

"I know. I just wanted to see for sure."

After another round of burgers and fries and

shakes we sat back and talked some more.

"How come you kept it a secret?" I asked.

"I tried to tell you, but you didn't listen. And you saw how mad Dad got about the motorbike. Think what he and Mom would do if they knew about all of this. Grown-ups don't understand about magic."

"Yeah," I agreed. "Mom and Dad wouldn't understand about this at all. They'd take away the cube and lock it up someplace, I bet."

Jeff's face got a tight look. "Nobody's ever going to do that," he said. "Nobody's going to take this magic cube away from me, *ever*."

"Calm down," I said. "It'll stay a secret just between you and me. Let's think of some more things to wish for."

Dad's voice broke into my words.

"Bill? Jeff? Come down for supper, boys."

"Oh my gosh!" I whispered. "He's on his way up here! What'll we do with all this stuff?"

"Wish it away quick," Jeff answered. "We can wish it back anytime we want to."

I felt dumb not to have figured that out myself.

We wished everything away in a hurry. I

wanted to keep wearing the purple sneakers, but I didn't know how I'd handle Mom's questions when she saw them. So the sneakers went too, and the digital watch, and all the comic books and the sports stuff and the video game. Everything.

The doorknob rattled.

"Boys? Supper's on. And it's your favorite, hamburgers and french fries."

"We'll be right there," Jeff called cheerfully.

He flipped the cube up into the air and caught it in one hand.

"I'd better take this along," he whispered to me with a grin. "Might have to wish supper away when they're not looking!"

FOUR

I was much too excited to sleep that night. I rolled around in bed for hours, thinking of all the things I could have anytime I wished for them with Jeff's cube.

Super Bowl tickets! Our whole family could go, and all my friends too.

That expensive new catcher's mitt Danny was saving up for! I could get it for him easily. The hard part would be not telling him how.

And new cars for Mom and Dad! I'd have to figure out some way to explain without getting into the kind of mess Jeff stirred up with his motorbike. Maybe I'd tell them I won the cars in a lottery, or something like that.

Finally I just couldn't stay in bed one minute longer. It wasn't even five o'clock, but I got up and went down the hall to Jeff's room.

"Wake up," I whispered. "Let's go to the playground."

"What for?" he mumbled sleepily.

"To look for another cube, so we can each have one of our own. Come on, and be quiet. Don't wake Mom and Dad."

The sun wasn't even up over the trees yet, and of course there wasn't anyone at the playground but the two of us. Jeff showed me exactly where he'd found the cube, and we started searching. There wasn't a clump of weeds or a clod of scuffed-up earth we didn't poke into. Now I know what people mean when they talk about leaving no stone unturned. We must have turned over hundreds of stones, but we didn't find any more cubes.

Jeff flopped down on one of the picnic benches. "Let's go home," he said. "We can get some videotapes, lots of cartoons, and—"

"No, wait," I said. "I just got an idea. Give me the cube."

Jeff fished it out of his pocket and handed it over. I closed my hand around it and waited till I had my thoughts all worked out. Then, very slowly and very carefully, I said, "If there are any more wishing cubes on this playground, or anyplace else, I wish they would pile up right here on this picnic table."

I held my breath, and so did Jeff. Nothing happened. The table was as empty as it had been before my wish.

"Okay, that does it," I said, and my breath came out like a long sigh. "I guess this really is the only one."

"I better not lose it ever," Jeff said. "Who do you suppose lost it here?"

Who would be so careless as to lose such a valuable thing? I wondered. Who would have such a thing in the first place?

Suddenly Jeff shouted, "Hey! I know what we can do! Let's *wish* for another one! Tell the cube to make another one!"

"Like a clone!" I shouted.

And with the cube clutched tightly in my fist

and my other hand open, palm up, I wished. "I wish this cube would make another wishing cube, just like this one."

It didn't. My other hand was still empty.

Jeff reached for the cube. "Let me try. I'm the one who found it." He wished the same wish, and the same thing happened. Nothing.

I guess we both had the same thought at the same time, but Jeff said it out loud, in a worried kind of way.

"That's twice it didn't do anything. Maybe it isn't working anymore."

"It has to," I said. "It just has to. Wish for something easy. Hurry up."

Jeff looked down at the cube and stammered, "I wish . . . uh, I wish for breakfast, a big breakfast!"

Pow! A whole meal appeared on the picnic table—a big platter of scrambled eggs, stacks of pancakes dripping with melted butter and syrup, muffins, strawberry jam, and a huge pitcher of orange juice.

"It still works!" Jeff shouted. "Let's eat!"

He dug into the food fast. I was hungry too, but I took my time. I had some thinking to do.

"Listen, Jeff," I said between bites of pancake. "Now we know something important about the cube."

"Yeah, it still works great!"

"No, I mean really important. So far it has done everything we've asked it to, except bring us another cube, right?"

"Right."

"So maybe that doesn't mean there aren't any more cubes anyplace. Maybe it means there's some crazy rule that says cubes can't move each other around."

"You mean there *might* be more of them someplace?"

"Sure, there might be lots of them. But this cube can't bring any of them to us."

"Do you suppose there's some other kid someplace who gets stuff by wishing?"

"Could be. But don't look so worried. Even if there is, he can't wish your cube away from you. That kind of wish doesn't work. We just proved it."

"So my cube will never get away from me, ever," Jeff said happily. "Hold it for a minute, will you? I'm going to finish the muffins."

I turned the cube around in my fingers, admiring its smooth, cool surface.

Would I ever like to know more about you, I thought. I sure wish I had some clues to this mystery.

There was a sudden crackling noise in my ears, as if I were wearing headphones with a loose wire. In between the static I heard men's voices.

"This one's going to be tougher," one voice said. "It's a couple of kids."

"Kids!" a second voice said. Then it faded away, but when I shook my head it came in again. ". . . proof?"

"Nothing solid," the first man answered, "but there's . . . and the instruments have been going crazy."

Maybe I was going crazy too. I looked over at Jeff. "Do you hear a radio?" I asked him.

"Nope. Pass the jam, will you?"

I glanced around. There was no one on the playground but us. No men talking. No radio. Still, the voices went on.

". . . get a team down to you fast," the second man was saying.

47

"No . . . not the way to handle it. Got to go at it without force . . . Give me a couple of days . . . think I can work something out."

"Okay, but no more than that," the second man answered. Crackles of static fuzzed out his next words, but then I could pick up a little more. " . . . risky to wait longer . . . what might happen if . . ."

Jeff gave me a poke. "Cut the daydreaming, will you? Three times I asked you to hand over the cube!"

"Oh . . . yeah, sure. What's up?"

"Breakfast's over, that's what. Okay, cube, I wish all these dirty dishes and leftovers would go away."

Poof! The picnic table was empty again. There was nothing to show what a wonderful breakfast had been there except the taste of maple syrup in my mouth and a smear of strawberry jam on Jeff's chin.

"C'mon!" he yelled. "Let's have some fun! Cube, I wish I had a basketball. And I wish I could make a basket every time."

As we ran over to the basketball court I

grabbed the cube and wished the same thing. Was it ever fun shooting baskets that way! We sank one-handers, and we whirled around backward and flipped the balls in without even looking.

After a while, though, it got boring sinking a basket every time we shot, and Jeff said, "There's nothing more to do here. Let's go home and wish back some of the stuff from yesterday."

"No, wait," I said. "There is something else."

Could the cube really do it? I wondered to myself. And if it could, did I dare?

"Aw, let's go," Jeff said impatiently. "Why are you standing there with a stupid look on your face?"

I made up my mind. I squeezed the cube and said, "I wish I could fly!"

Instantly I was jerked off my feet and thrust up into the air. It was a terrible feeling. I thrashed around, with my arms and legs flapping in all directions. Over and over I rolled, until finally I managed to straighten myself out and float on my stomach about twenty feet off

49

the ground. I fought off a dizzy, seasick feeling and looked down.

Jeff was running around, yelling excitedly. I waved one hand at him and felt myself rise a few feet on that side. Cautiously I waved the other hand. Sure enough, my body tilted to that side and up I went.

Now that I had more control, the dizziness went away.

"This is fun!" I shouted. "Watch me go!"

A waggle of the arms and up I went. Rolling over onto my right side, I pretended to be swimming the sidestroke. It felt funny not having any water to push against, but it worked. Off I sailed, right arm extending, left arm bending at the elbow, legs drawing up and pushing out again.

I managed a wobbly turn and floated back.

"Come down! Come down!" Jeff was jumping up and down trying to grab me, but I was too high. "I want to do it too!"

I thought about throwing the cube down to him, but I was afraid that without it I might go crashing down. So I yelled back, "Wait a minute! Your turn soon!"

I brought my legs up to my chest in a tight tuck, then shot them out behind me. *Zoom!* As I went skimming off again I could feel my shirt flap around me. This was the greatest!

I tried a back somersault, but made a mess of it. My arms and legs got all tangled up and it took a while to get them sorted out. I ended up floating belly down like a human blimp, and I decided to stick to plain swimming strokes. Some fast kicking and breaststroking sent me sailing out over the baseball diamond.

"Hey, Jeff! Come on over and see the world's craziest ball game!" I shouted.

I floated out to the pitcher's mound and waited for him to run to the diamond. "It's the last of the ninth, folks, and the score is six to three. The bases are loaded and the count is three and two, with two outs. It's a terrific battle between Bill Hasting, the sensational powerhouse pitcher, and Bill Hasting, the greatest slugger since Babe Ruth! And here comes the pitch!"

I doubled myself into a tuck, shot my legs out, and zoomed straight toward the batter's box like a pitched ball.

"It's a fast ball, folks, but Hasting connects. *Whap!*"

Without stopping I whipped around the plate and shot off toward first base. I could hear Jeff laughing and cheering as I made the turn and whizzed off toward second. Hey, I thought, I'm getting pretty good at this!

I did a quick flip around second and flew over to third with the air whipping my shirt and slamming up against my face. It felt great.

"Yay, Hasting! Come on, Bill Hasting!" Jeff shouted.

I swooped around third and zoomed down the baseline. "Folks, it's the home run of the century!" I yelled, and I threw my hands up into the air in triumph. And then—*wham!* My whole body followed my hands and snapped upward.

"Hey . . . hey!" I screamed. I was out of control and heading right for the tall trees at the edge of the ball diamond. I tried to slow down, to dive past the trees, to turn aside, to do anything—but it was too late. I went crashing through the leafy branches of a tall oak.

The branches scraped and pulled at me till

my feet finally connected with one that held me. I clung there, my heart thumping wildly and my stomach lurching, thirty or forty feet above the ground.

Jeff came running over. "That was great!" he shouted. "Now come down! It's my turn!"

I couldn't move. I could hardly catch my breath. It's okay, everything's okay, I kept telling myself as I tried to stop the pounding in my chest. As soon as I get my balance, I'll fly down nice and easy. No problem, no problem at all. Just another second or two, if I can only get my arm around this branch . . .

It was as far as I got, for just then a man's voice called, "Hey, up there! Need some help?"

Startled, I looked down. Standing next to Jeff was a youngish sort of man in green and yellow warm-up pants, a sweat shirt, and running shoes. Where had he come from all of a sudden? Had he seen me fly? What was I going to do now! I couldn't fly down right in front of him. Darn! What a rotten time for a Sunday-morning jogger to come along.

Maybe I could talk him into going away. "Thanks a lot," I shouted, "but, uh, I'm not coming down just yet. I . . . um, y'see, I'm . . . up here looking for my kite."

What a dopey thing to say. Nobody would be out flying a kite on a day like this one, without any wind. Well, it was the only thing I could think of. Maybe he'd buy it.

"Nice day for jogging," I added quickly.

"Sure is," he shouted back. "And a nice day for flying . . . kites!"

Oh boy, I groaned to myself. Did he see the whole thing?

He didn't say anything more, though. He just stood there, legs wide apart, hands on his hips, squinting up at me.

How long is this guy going to hang around? I wondered uneasily. It would only take one wish for the cube to get me down safely, but I didn't dare make that wish with him right there watching. And if I tried to get down on my own, without the cube's help, I'd be in for a bunch of broken arms and legs for sure.

I wish this guy would get out of here, I thought angrily.

All of a sudden a high-pitched beeping sound started up across the street from the

playground. It was coming from a blue van parked at the curb.

The jogger shot another look up at me, then ran over to the van. He pulled open the door on the driver's side and reached in. The beeping stopped.

I didn't wait another second. With one quick wish I was back down on the ground—flat on my bottom, but safely down.

"My turn now," Jeff said. "Gimme the cube."

"Shut up! That nosy jogger is coming back."

"How did you get down so fast?" said the jogger. "Last time I looked, you were up there with the squirrels."

I made a big production of brushing off my jeans so I wouldn't have to look him in the eye.

"I slid," I said. "C'mon, Jeff—we've got to get home. So long, mister." I gave Jeff a shove and we started off across the ball diamond.

And didn't that guy walk right along with us, as if he were our best buddy or something.

"I see you didn't find your kite," he said. "Too bad."

"Yeah . . . well, it's okay. I've got another one at home," I mumbled.

What was with him? Why didn't he leave us alone?

"Well, so long," I said again. "See you around."

"Yes," he answered kind of slowly. "I think you will."

Then he tossed a smile at us, ran back to the blue van, and drove away.

As the van turned the corner I said to Jeff, "Did you see the weird stuff on top of that van?"

Jeff shrugged. "Maybe the guy's a CB radio nut. Hand over the cube so I can fly too."

"Too late," I said. "Here comes Mr. Santori walking his dog."

A minute later the Greenberg twins ran into the playground and started playing on the swings, and pretty soon there were kids all over the place.

"C'mon," Jeff pestered. "I want my turn."

"Are you crazy? You want all these kids to find out our secret? We'd better go home."

"That's not fair. It's my cube!"

He pestered most of the way home, but I wouldn't give him the cube. I was afraid he'd do something dumb.

I tried to tune out his voice so I could think about the man in the playground and that van of his. Sure, a lot of people around town had CB stuff in their cars, but they didn't have anything like the stuff on top of that van—a big loop antenna going around and around, and something else that looked like the radar receivers I'd seen pictures of in news magazines.

I was still thinking about it when we got to our house. The Sunday-morning paper was sitting on the front steps.

"Me first with the funnies!" Jeff hollered. He made a dive for the paper and stuck his tongue out at me as he slammed into the house.

I didn't care. For once the funnies weren't important at all. I went inside slowly, wondering a crazy thought.

Was there . . . could there possibly be some sort of connection between the jogger and the cube?

FIVE

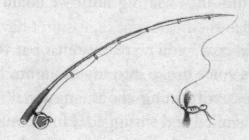

At school the next morning I tried to act as if I'd had just an ordinary weekend like everyone else. The kids in my class were all jabbering about their ball games and picnics and visits with relatives, but I kept quiet.

Would their eyes ever bug out if they knew what Jeff and I had done!

But they weren't going to know. We had decided to keep the cube a secret from everybody, even our best friends.

Before leaving for school that morning we'd

hidden the cube way in the back of Jeff's closet, and we'd made a plan. We would hurry right home after school and try to find a place where Jeff could fly without being seen. He was just about busting to fly, and I had a hard time talking him into waiting until we could figure out some—

"Holy cow, you're really out of it today!" Danny's voice broke into my thoughts. "What are you daydreaming about, anyway?"

I just smiled and shrugged. How could I tell him that my head was a jumble of video games and mile-high stacks of comic books and purple sneakers and food that appeared out of nowhere—and flying!

I was foggy headed all through math and science, but it was one of those lucky days when I didn't get called on in class. Then at lunchtime something happened that shook me wide awake.

Danny and Frank and I were standing in the milk line when Jeff's class came into the cafeteria. As soon as Jeff saw me he came running over.

"Guess what!" he shouted. The milk money lady glared at him for busting into the line, and I glared at him too. What was he going to spill about our secret?

"Guess what!" he said again. "We have a new gym teacher!"

Whew! Was that all? "So what?" I said. "Mr. Willis out sick?"

"No, he's gone!"

"What do you mean, gone?" asked Frank as he put a carton of milk on his tray. "He coached Little League practice in the park yesterday. I saw him."

"Well he's gone now," Jeff insisted. "We have a new gym teacher. This new guy said he's taking Mr. Willis's place. And listen, Bill—it's the man in the playground!"

I almost dropped my tray.

"That's crazy," I said. "It couldn't be."

But it was. That afternoon when my class went to gym I saw that Jeff had been right. It *was* the man from the playground, right down to the same green and yellow warm-up pants and sweat shirt. Now he had Mr. Willis's whistle around his neck, and as soon as we all came out of the locker room he blew it and told us to line up facing him.

"My name is Mr. Jackson," he said. "I want you all to call me Coach."

"Where's Mr. Willis?" somebody asked.

"Mr. Willis won't be in school for a while," he answered.

"How long's he gonna be gone?" asked Danny.

This Coach fellow didn't answer right away. "Hard to tell," he finally said. "It all depends."

Not much of an answer, I thought. It got harder to shove away my uneasy feeling about him.

He checked the class list in his hand and started walking down the line, looking carefully at everybody. I was hoping he wouldn't recognize me, but he did. He stopped and read aloud the name on my gym shirt.

"Hasting," he said. "The kite flyer."

Then he winked at me. I suppose it would have been cool to wink back, but I didn't.

Well, he sure wasn't much of a gym teacher. All he did was toss out a batch of basketballs and have us practice free shots. He joked a lot, though, and all the kids seemed to like him. All except me. I felt as if he were watching me more than anyone else. He seemed surprised every time I muffed a shot. Believe me, I was glad when gym was over and I could get out of there.

Jeff and I raced home, full of plans about flying. Mom met us at the door.

"Let's go, boys," she said.

"Go where?"

"Did you forget? Today's the day I promised to take you shopping for Dad's birthday present. Hurry up and grab a quick snack so we can get going. I have to finish Mrs. Randall's wall hanging."

We *had* forgotten. Dad's birthday was the next day. We'd been saving up our allowances to get him a fishing rod, and Mom had said she'd take us to the sports store at the mall.

"Aw, gee," Jeff said. "Do we have to?"

My elbow in his ribs shut him up. I had a great idea!

"Tell you what," I said to Mom. "Jeff and I will take care of the whole thing ourselves. You stay here and we'll take the bus downtown to Parson's and that'll give you plenty of time to finish up the wall hanging."

"Oh, honey," Mom said, "Parson's is much more expensive than the store at the mall."

"We'll make out just fine," I said quickly. "I heard they're having a sale. C'mon, Jeff. Let's go up and get, you know—our money!"

It didn't take much to persuade Mom, but I had a hard time with Jeff.

"What's the matter with you?" he said as soon as we got up to his room. "Why'd you tell her that? We don't have to waste time going downtown. All we have to do is wish for the rod."

"What's the matter with *you*?" I snapped back. "How are we going to explain having Dad's present without going shopping for it? And what if he doesn't like it? What if it's the wrong kind? How would he take it back without a sales slip? Did you ever think of that?"

"No, but . . ."

"Listen, what we'll do is go to Parson's, pick out a rod, and wish for the money. That way it'll be just like buying something the ordinary

64

way. C'mon, get the cube and let's go."

"But there won't be time for me to fly if we go shopping. Can't we do it the other way?"

"No, we can't. Now stop pestering and come on."

A little while later Jeff and I were on the bus heading downtown, and I had another idea.

"Listen!" I said. "We're going to get Dad the very best rod in the whole store, right?"

"I s'pose," Jeff said grumpily.

"Well, how about this? Why stop at just one? The cube'll give us as much money as we wish for. So let's get four rods—one for each of us!"

"Yeah! Then we can all go fishing together!"

After that Jeff perked up. We spent the rest of the ride downtown planning what to buy and talking about how great it would be for us all to have some family fishing trips. Maybe next Saturday we'd all drive out to the lake. Jeff and I would think up some good stuff to do out there with the cube while Mom and Dad weren't watching!

There was one problem. Parson's was right next door to Dad's bank.

"What if he sees us coming out of there with

the present? Then it won't be a surprise," Jeff said.

I thought for a minute and decided we'd have to take a chance. "He'll probably be in his office," I said. "Bank managers don't stand around looking out the window."

Well, we got to Parson's and we picked out four great fishing rods and the reels and other stuff to go with them—hooks and leaders and spinners and flies and a couple of fish-cleaning knives and all kinds of things. The clerk kept looking at us as if he didn't expect we could pay for it all.

"You boys sure you want all this gear?" he asked. "It's going to add up to a lot of money."

"Sure we're sure," I answered. "Just put it in two packages so we can carry it home. Oh, and we want them gift wrapped, please." I may have sounded confident, but inside I was wondering nervously if the cube would come through. In spite of all our wishing, we had never asked it for money before. Maybe we should have tried it out before getting into this.

"That comes to $146.85," said the clerk. "Plus $7.35 sales tax. That'll be $154.20 alto-

gether. Have you got that much?"

Jeff and I looked at each other. Now what? We couldn't just stand there and make the money appear right in front of this man's eyes.

I groaned to myself. We should have planned this better.

This time Jeff thought faster than I did. "Mister," he said politely, "can I please use your bathroom?"

The clerk gave Jeff a funny look, but he pointed to a door and said, "Over there, sonny. Turn the handle to the right."

"I better go with him," I said quickly, and we both scooted into the men's room and leaned against the door in case anyone else tried to get in. Jeff pulled the cube out of his pocket.

"Okay, cube, do your stuff," he said. "I wish for $154.20."

The money piled up in his hand—a big batch of bills and a lot of coins. I had to catch the overflow.

"This is great!" I said. "It even looks like we saved it up ourselves!"

The clerk's eyebrows went up when he counted the money and found that it came out to just the right amount, but he didn't say anything.

We each took a package and walked out as casually as we could. On the way I heard the clerk say to one of the others, "Harry, you'll never believe the crazy sale I just made. There were these two kids with their hands full of money . . ."

We didn't dare laugh until we were back on the bus going home.

It was almost time for dinner, but Mom was still clanking away at her loom so it was easy to get upstairs and stow the packages in Jeff's closet. We put the cube away too, very carefully.

"Just think!" I said. "We can do a lot of good things with this cube. We can give money to all the poor people in town."

"We can give the Community Center money to build a new pool," Jeff said excitedly. "And we can buy tons of Girl Scout cookies!"

"And Dad will never have to raise our allowances 'cause we can wish ourselves spending money whenever we want it!"

"You dummy! Why would we ever need

spending money? The cube can get us anything we want. Anything in the whole world! *Yowie!*"

He punched me and I poked him back and we rolled around on the floor, whooping and hollering and laughing. I wondered how we'd ever be able to keep our faces straight during dinner. I was sure that every time we looked at each other we'd bust out laughing and cheering. Then how long could we keep the whole thing a secret from Mom and Dad?

But I didn't need to worry. Dad phoned from the bank to say he couldn't get home for dinner, so Mom let Jeff and me eat in front of the TV while she went back to her weaving.

When it got to be eight o'clock and Dad still wasn't home, Mom called the bank to see what was the matter. Jeff and I were at the refrigerator getting ourselves some milk and we heard her talking to Dad on the kitchen phone. When she hung up she looked puzzled, and a little bit worried.

"Is something wrong with Dad?" I asked.

"Oh no, honey," she said quickly. "It's just

some sort of mix-up at the bank and he can't leave till it's all straightened out."

"What kind of mix-up?"

"Well, you know that every day things have to balance at a bank. The money withdrawn and the money people deposit—every transaction is written down and fed into the computer and then tallied at the end of the day. And today, at the final tally, the bank was short some money. I think Dad said it was $154.20."

Crash! That was Jeff dropping his glass of milk. I wasn't too steady myself. I grabbed a wad of paper towels, and as we bent down over the puddle of milk he and I looked at each other. I guess I was as pale as he was.

Mom didn't notice. She checked to make sure we were getting all the broken glass up and weren't cutting ourselves, and then she went to stir the stew she was keeping warm for Dad.

"What's going to happen?" I asked.

She sighed. "I guess the people who work at the bank will have to stay and keep checking until the error shows up, or maybe until someone owns up to taking the money."

"Did they call the police?" Jeff asked in a small voice.

"No, not for such a small amount of money. Don't worry, they'll get it all settled. It's only a hundred and fifty dollars."

"A hundred and fifty-*four* dollars," Jeff corrected unhappily. "And twenty cents."

It didn't do Jeff and me any good to stand there staring at each other. I pulled him out of the kitchen. We dashed upstairs and locked the door of his room behind us.

SIX

I sat down on the bed and tried to figure things out.

"What's it all mean?" Jeff wailed. "Did the cube steal the money from Dad's bank?"

"How should I know?" I snapped. "Shut up a minute and let me think."

What kind of hokey trick had the cube pulled? I thought angrily. Getting the money right out of our own father's bank, next door to Parson's! Well, it could put it right back, that's what.

I poked Jeff. "It's okay," I told him. "All we have to do is wish the money back to the bank and everything'll be fine."

"You mean wish it out of Parson's cash register? That's no good."

He was right. We had the fishing gear, so the money had to stay at Parson's. What a mess!

"Look," I said finally, "it's not our problem. Let the cube take care of it. All *we* have to do is wish the money to be back in the bank—but not taken away from Parson's—and the whole thing will be fixed up, somehow."

So that's what we wished. And about an hour later Dad came home.

He sat at the kitchen table and picked at the supper Mom had kept warm for him. He looked tired, and sort of cross.

"Everything okay now, Dad?" I asked cheerfully.

"Not really. I have to get back to the bank soon."

Jeff shot me a look that said "Now what?" I wondered too, but it was Mom who asked, "What do you mean? What's going on?"

Dad sighed. "We've been going around

74

in circles for hours," he said. "It's not a lot of money, but everything has to balance at the end of the day, and today—well, I've never seen anything like what happened today." He shook his head and took another sip of coffee.

We all waited for him to go on.

"There we were, checking and rechecking each teller's cash box against all the deposit and withdrawal slips, and we kept coming up short $154.20 every time. And it was all so strange."

"Strange? How?" Mom asked.

"We had four tellers working today. What is strange is that there was exactly the same amount of money missing from each teller's cash box. Four tellers, each with $38.55 missing!"

"That *is* unusual," Mom said.

"And that's not all. How do you figure this? Not ten minutes after I talked to you tonight the money was back in the cash boxes!"

Thanks, cube, I thought. I wonder how you did it without taking it away from Parson's.

"Well then," Mom said with a sigh of relief. "Now it's all straightened out."

75

"No it isn't," Dad said. "Not at all. The money's there, but something really strange is going on."

I groaned. What now?

"We were doing our last count when all of

a sudden the computers started up. Banking hours were over, and yet the computers were making transactions at top speed."

"Who turned them on?" Jeff asked.

"Nobody turned them on, Jeff. They were shut down for the day."

I could picture the computers suddenly humming away, their screens lit up with fast-moving numbers. I could picture Dad and the others standing there, watching in amazement. I began to feel uncomfortable again.

"So what?" Jeff said impatiently. "What difference does it make? The money's back."

Dad took another gulp of coffee. "No, Jeff. The money isn't back at all. Now it's gone in a different way."

It was getting too complicated for me. I pulled my chair closer to Dad. "I don't get it," I said. "You said the money turned up in the tellers' cash boxes."

"It did. Actual cash—bills and change, all adding up to the missing $154.20. But when the computers finally stopped and we could take a close look at the printouts, we discovered that what they had been doing was subtracting three cents from every single one of our depositors' accounts."

"*Three cents?* How come?"

"Figure it out, Bill. The bank has 5,140 accounts, and each one now has three cents less than it did. What does it all add up to?"

He took a pencil out of his shirt pocket and started writing numbers on a piece of paper, but I didn't look. I knew what the answer would be.

Jeff peered over Dad's shoulder. "Oh my gosh!" he said. "It comes out to $154.20!"

"I don't understand this whole thing," Mom said.

"Neither do I," Dad said. "And neither does the squad of computer engineers I had to call in."

"What's going to happen now?" Jeff asked. He slid his eyes around to me as he spoke.

Dad stood up and put his suit coat back on. "We'll work it out somehow. I have to get back down there and see if they've made any progress." He smiled at Jeff and me and said, "It's nice of you boys to be so interested, but don't worry. It's probably a crossed circuit in the computers somewhere."

"What if . . . what if it isn't?" Jeff wanted to know.

"Well, it's not a large amount of money. If we can't find the error, we'll just find some way to take the loss and balance the accounts. What bothers me is that we're going to end up spending about eight hundred dollars in overtime pay for the tellers and engineers—and all for a hundred and fifty dollars."

"A hundred and fifty-*four* dollars, and twenty cents," Jeff corrected again, and he sounded so woeful that Dad chuckled.

"Right on the nose, son," he said. "Now you fellas go up to bed. It's late. And don't be upset about any of this. It's not your worry."

As he kissed Mom good-bye Jeff and I stared at each other. Not our worry? That's what *he* thought.

We did go upstairs, but we didn't go to bed. We sat in Jeff's room and went through the whole thing once more. Slowly I tried to fit the pieces together.

"Step One, we wished for the money," I

79

said. "Step Two, we got it. But why did the money come from Dad's bank?"

Neither of us had an answer for that. But I started thinking about all the other stuff we'd wished for. Had that come from real places too?

If it had, then . . .

"Jeff! I've got it figured out! It's teleportation!"

Jeff looked blank. "Tell-a-what?"

"Tel-e-por-tation," I repeated. "It means moving things from one place to another so fast you can't see it happen. So that's how the cube works!"

"But I thought the cube sort of made stuff out of nothing," Jeff said.

"Me too, but I guess it doesn't. When you wish for something, it teleports it to you, faster than you can see."

"I get it," Jeff said. "When we wished for the money at Parson's, it tel . . . it moved the money out of the bank and into our hands. Then tonight we wished it back and the tellers' cash boxes got filled up so fast that nobody saw it happen."

"Right! And I thought teleportation was

something people made up for science fiction books!"

"But, Bill—where did the tellers' money come from? We told the cube not to take it away from Parson's."

"That's where the crazy computers come in. Don't you see? The cube got the tellers' money out of the bank's reserve cash in the vault. So then the computers had to change the records of each person's account to make up for the shortage of cash in the vault. Get it?"

"I guess so," he said slowly. "But what about the cartoons at the movie? And the way you flew? Was all that tellsportation too?"

"I don't know. And right now it doesn't matter. What we've got to do quick is figure out how to get Dad out of this mess at the bank."

"Easy. Tell the cube to fix the records. Tell it to add three cents back to each of the bank accounts."

"That won't work. It'll have to move the money from someplace else—maybe from some other bank!"

We were both quiet for a long while. I felt

as if we were tangled up in a huge pile of snarled string. And I began to see that no matter what we might wish, there was no way to cover that $154.20 without making the snarls worse and worse.

"Listen, Jeff," I said slowly, "there's only one thing to do."

When I told him what it was, he looked as if he were going to cry.

I didn't feel so great myself as we pulled the brightly wrapped packages out of the closet.

He handed me the cube. "Here, you do it. I don't want to."

So I did it. I wished Dad's birthday present back to Parson's. All that wonderful fishing gear. All those wonderful Saturdays at the lake.

It took some complicated wishing, because it had to look as if the stuff had never been bought in the first place. We had to undo the gift wrapping and take everything out of the boxes and then wish each separate thing back into Parson's stock. Then I wished back the empty boxes, and at the very end I wished back the sales slip, after carefully wishing the clerk's writing off of it.

"Okay, that's that," I said. "It's just as if we'd never bought it at all."

"What about the clerk?" Jeff said. "Won't he remember he sold it to us?"

"Well, maybe he won't notice it's back. Besides, even if he does, it's all so crazy who'd believe him anyhow?"

The last thing I did was wish the money out of Parson's and back to the bank, *really* back, so that all the accounts would be straight again.

When it was all finished, Jeff and I sat on the floor gloomily.

"It sure would have been a great birthday present," he said with a sigh.

Neither of us said anything for a long time. Then Jeff asked, "Can we ever wish for money, Bill? Ever again?"

"Probably not. It's so complicated."

Good-bye, Community Center Swimming Pool, I thought to myself. And I'm sorry, really sorry, all you poor people. Now you'll never have all that money we were going to give you.

We were both too downcast to talk about it anymore. After a while Jeff said, "I'm hungry. Let's go get a snack."

Slowly we went downstairs again. Mom was in the living room, wandering around as if she didn't quite know what to do. I saw her fuss a bit with Dad's rock collection, picking up a geode and a piece of amethyst crystal, rubbing off a bit of dust, then putting them down again. I guess she was trying to relax, but it didn't seem to be helping much.

Jeff and I were into our second handfuls of raisins when she came into the kitchen.

"There's been so much commotion tonight I forgot to ask you," she said. "Did you boys get the fishing rod for Dad?"

Jeff ducked his head so I knew it was up to me, but I didn't know what to say.

"No, not exactly, no, we didn't," I stammered. "It was . . . there wasn't . . . uh, they didn't have the kind we wanted."

"Too bad. Well then, what *did* you get him?"

"I . . . we . . . uh, well, it's a surprise. We can't tell you what it is." I tried to look as if I knew what I was talking about.

"Whatever it is," Mom said with a smile, "I'm sure Dad will love it. We'll give him our

84

gifts at breakfast tomorrow. Now scoot off to bed, both of you."

We scooted—right back to Jeff's room to tackle this newest problem.

"Now what'll we do?" I said.

"*Now* ask the cube to get us something for him, just like I wanted to do in the first place only you were so smart you had to have us go shopping and wish for money and get everything messed up."

"Well we can mess up again if we're not careful," I shot back. "Maybe we shouldn't take a chance on another hassle by wishing for something else out of a store."

"Why not?" Jeff said. "There wasn't any hassle over all that good stuff we got—the video game and the skis and the comic books and everything."

"Not that we know about, anyway," I said. "It's just that I have this feeling. I can't explain it because there's too much to figure out, but what if everything we wish for has to be accounted for in some way? What if . . . ?"

"You worry too much," Jeff snapped. "And besides, what else can we do? Where are we going to dig up a present for Dad that doesn't come from a store?"

"That's it!" I cried. "We'll dig it up!"

"Huh?"

"We'll wish for a rock for his collection—a rock right out of the ground! *That* won't mess up a store or a bank or anything!"

Jeff caught on. "Yeah! A rock from some faraway place where nobody will even know it's gone. I'll get the cube!"

We were very careful about this wish. First we sneaked downstairs and got some of Dad's books about rocks and minerals. We looked through the pages, trying to pick out just the right specimen. Jeff had trouble reading most of the names, but I helped him.

"Rubellite . . . pegmatite . . . no, those are no good. They come from mountains. Might start an avalanche."

"How about this one . . . marcasite?"

"No, it's found mostly in caves. If the cube pulls a chunk out of a place like that it could start a cave-in."

"Are you ever a worrywart! Here's a nice one. What's it called?"

86

"Aragonite," I read. "No, it's too rare. Dad would ask us all kinds of questions about where we got it, and he'd know it costs a lot of money in a rock shop."

"I'm tired," Jeff complained. "This is boring. Let's let the cube choose."

"No way! It might bring us a diamond or an emerald, and then what would we do! Just keep looking."

Finally we found it. "Listen to this," I said. " 'Round, petal-shaped rosettes of barite crystals abound in the sandy regions of the American west. Many a collector has come upon a lovely specimen of such a desert rose lying on the ground.' That's it! Just lying around! Let's get one of these!"

I grabbed the cube and made the wish. *Thunk!* There in the middle of Jeff's floor was a large, pale red hunk of rock. It did look a little like a rose, and some of its "petals" were still covered with bits of sand.

"Dad'll love it! Quick—let's wrap it up!"

We found some tissue paper, wrapped the rock carefully, and wrote HAPPY BIRTH-DAY, DAD in Magic Marker. Then we stashed the present under Jeff's bed, and I went back to my room.

I couldn't sleep, though. There were too many things to think about and wonder about, too many questions I couldn't answer, and that strange, uneasy feeling that wouldn't go away.

A couple of hours later I heard Dad come home. Mom had waited up for him, and as they came upstairs I could hear him telling her that things at the bank were okay now.

"Everything's straightened out, finally. The engineers think it was a temporary computer glitch of some kind. There's no other explanation."

"But how did it happen?" Mom asked.

"Nobody knows," Dad said wearily. "The power company's been having a lot of trouble lately, so maybe . . . I don't know. I just hope it never happens again."

"I do too," Mom said. "And I'm so glad everything's all right now."

But was it? Everything? I lay in bed and stared up at the ceiling. And again I began to wonder if having this cube could mean trouble—big trouble.

SEVEN

...STRANGE...UNEXPLAINED...LAST SATURDAY...
...STRAND MOVIE THEA...AT THE...LIBR...
...MADAME PIRETTE'S DANCE...

We didn't get to give Dad his birthday present the next morning after all, because he left for work long before Jeff and I woke up. Mom told us there were still a lot of things he had to put in order before the bank could open for business.

So at breakfast it was just Mom and Jeff and me.

Jeff dug into his cornflakes without a word, and Mom sat with her hands wrapped around her mug of coffee. She looked tired.

I slid a couple of pieces of bread into the toaster, then turned on the radio.

The announcer was just finishing the world news. "And now for a look at the local scene," he said. "City officials continue to be baffled over reports of strange and apparently unexplained events that took place here in Clinton last Saturday. On that day, at the Strand movie theater, a showing of the feature film was mysteriously interrupted by cartoons, although no reel of cartoon film could be found anywhere in the projection room. According to the manager . . ."

Jeff's head snapped up. An alarm bell went off in me too.

". . . and later that same day more than two hundred comic books suddenly appeared on shelves at the Clinton Public Library. Startled librarians said that the library's collection has never included comic books and that none had been purchased. Meanwhile, on the other side of the city, small toy cars by the dozen began racing about the showroom of the Ace Auto Company, while at Madame Pirette's Dance Academy thirty-six pairs of size eight and a half sneakers unexpectedly turned up in the girls' dressing room, hanging by their laces next to the dancers' ballet slippers. No one seems to . . ."

"Hey!" Jeff said. "Do you think that's . . . ?"

I kicked him under the table. Sure it was our stuff, everything we'd wished away in such a hurry last Saturday.

Mom turned the radio up louder. "I don't believe a word of this," she said, laughing. "It must be a joke."

It was no joke. Not to the residents of the Old Folks Home who suddenly found their lounge cluttered with kids' toys and games. And not to the champion bridge players whose tournament broke up in confusion when baseball cards got mixed in with their bridge decks.

I felt my face turn hot as the announcer reported how a butcher on Jerome Street had found his freezer filled with hockey skates, goalie pads, and two complete sets of skis, ski boots, and ski poles.

"Police were called to the Clinton Heights mansion of Mr. and Mrs. Dewey Montclair," the voice went on, "to investigate the sudden appearance of a flashing, buzzing video game in the midst of a reception honoring the city's social leaders. Startled guests said . . ."

By now Jeff was just about falling off his chair laughing.

"Where do you suppose the TV went?" he asked.

"What TV?" Mom asked, but I shut Jeff up with another kick and pretended not to hear her.

That crazy cube. We'd wished everything away so fast that we hadn't given it clear enough instructions, so all of our stuff had turned up in weird places—everything.

I bet there weren't many towns like Clinton last Saturday, where the park's statue of an ancient Greek athlete had a tennis racket and a pair of purple sneakers tucked in the crook of its arm and a digital watch on its wrist.

"City officials stress that there is no cause for alarm. However, the mayor has called a meeting of the City Council at noon today to discuss this baffling situation. Meanwhile . . ."

I'd heard enough. I shoved away from the table and picked up my books.

"Must be some nut on the loose," I said.

"C'mon, Jeff. 'Bye, Mom—see you after school."

She blew a kiss at each of us and turned back to the radio. As we went out the door I could still hear the announcer.

"And now for the rest of the local news. Electric company crews are trying to locate the source of dimouts and power surges in some neighborhoods. There is concern that . . ."

I was glad to get away from the sound of his voice. The electric company's troubles were nothing compared with what Jeff and I had stirred up with the cube.

On the way to school Jeff kept laughing, but I cut him off.

"Listen," I said. "No more wishing for a while, okay?"

"But I want to fly!"

"Never mind what you want. There's an awful lot we don't know about the cube, so I don't think we should use it till we get some things figured out."

"But you said you *did* have it figured out. You said—"

"Yeah, I know what I said. Teleportation.

But look how it teleported everything all over town to such crazy places, as if it were doing its own thinking and trying to match up our stuff with places for it. Don't you see? The mess at the bank and now this. It's too risky to do any more wishing till we can handle it better."

"You worry too much," Jeff said angrily. "The cube got us the rock last night without any trouble, didn't it?"

"Jeff, listen!"

"No! It's *my* cube and it's *my* magic. And I'm going to go flying with it after school today, and you're not going to stop me. So just shut up!"

I shut up. There's no use arguing with a kid as stubborn as Jeff.

Magic, he'd said. Well, it was too much magic for us if we didn't learn to control it, soon.

At school I had another bad morning. I guess maybe I do worry a lot. Anyway, the day got worse, because when we got back from lunch there was a note on my desk. REPORT TO THE GYM AFTER DISMISSAL. It was signed, COACH JACKSON.

I looked around at Danny and Frank and the rest of the guys. "Hey," I said, "anybody else get one of these?"

Nobody had. I was the only one Coach Jackson wanted to see.

My stomach lurched with that same uneasy feeling I always seemed to get whenever I thought about this Coach fellow. There was just something about him that didn't feel quite right.

After dismissal I forced myself down the hall toward the gym. I was almost there when I saw Jeff coming the other way. He had a note from Coach too.

"What do you suppose he wants with us?" he asked.

"Who knows?" I tried to shrug and sound cool, but I sure didn't feel that way inside.

We pushed open the gym door a crack and peered in.

The gym was empty. With the lights off, it seemed big and shadowy, but we could see that equipment left over from the day's classes was all over the place. The place was a mess.

Mr. Willis always had each class put its

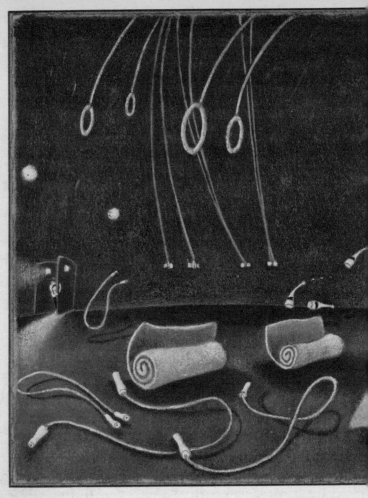

equipment away before leaving, but it looked as if this Coach guy had left the whole day's worth of stuff for himself to put away after school. That would be some job, I thought to

myself. What a stupid guy.

Or maybe . . . Sure, that was it! He wanted Jeff and me to help clean it up. Sure! Being new at school, he probably figured he knew us better than any of the other kids because he had met us at the playground.

My jumpiness eased off and I started to push the door wider. When I saw him come out of the gym office next to the bleachers, I don't know why but I shrank back against the doorway and pulled Jeff next to me, with my hand across his mouth just in case.

Coach didn't see us. He was looking at the mess in the gym—looking at it very carefully. Then he reached into the pocket of his warm-up jacket, and suddenly THE GYM STARTED TO CLEAN ITSELF UP!

Coach just stood there, not moving at all, but all around him everything else moved. The ropes and rings zoomed up to the ceiling and then their pulley ropes looped themselves around the wall hooks and fastened themselves down with firm little tugs. The tumbling mats rolled themselves up and slid into the storage space under the bleachers. The other stuff—all the balls and jump ropes and Indian clubs—went scooting across the floor, and then each thing jumped—yes, jumped!—into its own compartment of the storage bin. The cover of the bin swung over and slammed shut, and the latch snapped.

One perfect clean-up job, done in less than thirty seconds.

And Coach hadn't touched a thing himself.

Jeff wiggled out of my grip. His whisper was so loud it echoed across the whole gym.

"Bill! He's got a cube too!"

EIGHT

Coach spun around and saw us in the doorway. Let me tell you, I was scared. I didn't know whether to run or to stay.

He was cool, though. He smiled and said, "Hi, fellas. You're early. Come on in."

I hesitated, but Jeff went trotting right into the gym. I couldn't leave him alone with Coach so I went too. As we followed Coach into the office, curiosity shoved some of my fear aside.

Where had this guy found another cube?

Inside the office I began to feel uneasy again.

I'd been there lots of times, so I knew it wasn't the place that was giving me such a creepy feeling. There was Mr. Willis's old oak desk, still cluttered with score sheets and schedules and faculty notices. Beside the door stood the same tall, skinny first-aid cabinet, its white paint chipped off at the corners. There wasn't anything different—except this strange Coach guy. Once more I wondered who he really was, and what he wanted with us, and if he knew about our cube.

He closed the door and got right down to it.

"Okay, boys, let's level with each other. I know you have one of these." He shoved aside the papers on the desk and set down a small metal cube.

"That's just like mine!" Jeff said excitedly.

There was no use pretending anymore. "So you did see us," I said. "You saw what we did that day at the playground."

"Some of it." He grinned, but it didn't make me feel any more comfortable. "I got there in time to see you fly into that tree, Bill. Too bad. I could have saved you the crash landing if I'd tracked you kids there sooner."

Tracked us? Of course! The rotating antenna on top of his van. Dumb of me not to have figured out it was tracking equipment.

"Well, what's it all about?" I asked, hoping I sounded as cool as he did. "How does this teleportation stuff work anyway?"

He waved off my questions. "Hold it. First you two tell me this—who knows you have the cube? Your parents? Your friends?"

Jeff and I both shook our heads. "Nobody," I said.

"Good. I'm glad you haven't been busy showing off. That's good. Makes it easier."

He sat down behind the desk and beckoned to us. "Pull up that bench and sit down."

He seemed friendly enough, but I had a feeling there was trouble coming. As Jeff and I slung our legs over the bench I felt that same uneasiness.

I kept quiet while Jeff chattered away. "Is this some kind of club?" he asked eagerly. "All of us guys who have magic cubes could do lots of stuff together! You know what I'm gonna do next? I'm gonna fly! And then . . ."

Coach didn't pay any attention. He shot questions of his own right over Jeff's voice. He wanted to know exactly where we'd found the cube, and when, and how. Jeff calmed down enough to tell about it, and then I told about the things we'd done.

Coach already knew about the comic books and the sneakers and all the other stuff. "I heard the morning news," he said. "Figured you fellas were tangled up in all of that somehow."

The mix-up at Dad's bank was news to him, though. "Whew," he whistled after I finished describing what had happened there. "What a mess."

"It sure was," I agreed. "We didn't think wishing for money would be as complicated as that."

Then I decided to take a chance. "Listen," I began, "maybe you can help us. There must be a way we can wish for money without so much hassle. How about telling us how to do it?"

He leaned across the desk and shook his head.

"No, I'm afraid that's the end of it, boys," he

said. "I've got to have that cube back—right now."

My heart went bumping all the way down to my stomach. Not have the cube anymore?

"You got to be kidding!" Jeff cried.

"Sorry," Coach said. "I know it's tough, but you have to give it back."

"Forget it!" Jeff shouted as he jumped up. "I found it so it's mine—finders keepers! C'mon, Bill, let's get out of here!"

"Hold on a minute," I told Jeff. I said to Coach, "You mean it's your cube? You're the one who lost it in the playground?"

"Not exactly."

"See?" Jeff shouted. "He's trying to get something that isn't even his! No way! It's mine!"

"Cool down, Jeff," Coach said firmly. "Now sit down and listen."

Jeff threw himself onto the bench again, but he glared at Coach. "It's not fair. You've already got one cube. How much magic do you need, anyway?"

"Jeff," Coach said quietly, "the cube isn't magic."

Jeff gave him a sulky look. "Than how come it makes wishes come true? That's magic, isn't it?"

"I guess it seems that way. But you see, there are a lot of complicated things involved here, too complicated and dangerous for kids to fool around with."

"That's nuts," Jeff said. "My cube never hurt us a bit, right, Bill? Tell him it's not dangerous."

"You kids don't know what danger is," Coach said. He sounded impatient. "Look, even if it *were* your cube—even if I could let you keep it, suppose it got lost, or stolen. And suppose the person who got hold of it wanted more than comic books and video games."

"Like what?"

"Well, like huge amounts of money, for instance. You saw what happened at your dad's bank with just a hundred and fifty dollars. What would happen if somebody 'wished' millions of dollars out of banks everywhere?"

I thought hard. "That would be pretty terrible," I said.

"You bet it would. The banking system of the whole world would collapse. And think of all the people who would lose all the money they'd saved."

"But . . ."

"Or suppose something worse. What if the cube got into the hands of somebody who wanted power—power over other people, or over other countries. Maybe even power over the whole world. Think about that."

I was beginning to see what he was getting at. "You mean a person could be crazy, and use the cube to wreck a whole bunch of cities? That could start a war," I said slowly.

Coach nodded. "You've got it, Bill."

He turned to Jeff. "Do you see how dangerous the cube could be?"

Jeff doesn't give up easily. "Listen," he begged, "you don't have to worry about us losing the cube or anything like that. We take real good care of it. We don't carry it around with us. It's in a hiding place, and nobody knows we have it—not even Mom and Dad. And we won't tell anybody about it, ever. We'll keep it real safe, honest. None of those bad things will happen."

Coach shook his head. "Sorry," he said.

"You and your brother are into something you shouldn't be. I've got to have that cube."

Any other kid would have been crying now, I suppose, but not Jeff. His chin stuck out stubbornly and the freckles on his face disappeared under angry red splotches. He jumped up from the bench so fast that I almost fell over backward.

"No!" he yelled. "The cube's mine! You can't have it, ever! You're one of those bad guys yourself! I don't care what you say, the cube's MINE! You'll never get it!"

"Hold on, Jeff!" I shouted, but he was too far gone in rage to hear me. He yanked open the office door, still hollering.

"Never, never!" he howled at Coach. "And I'll fix it so you'll never bother me again! I'll get my cube and wish you far away! I'll wish you dead, that's what I'll wish! And you can't stop me!"

Coach made a grab for him, but it was too late. With both hands Jeff pulled over the tall first-aid cabinet. He jumped clear as it crashed down across the doorway, with splinters of its glass door flying in all directions and bottles of alcohol smashing onto the floor.

As he raced across the gym his shouts bounced off the walls.

"You can't stop me! You can't stop me! Drop dead!"

The big swinging doors of the gym swooshed open, and he was gone.

I shook the sound of crashing glass and metal out of my head.

"He's so mad he'll really do something terrible," I cried. "He's just a little kid!"

"Stubborn little kid," Coach muttered as he scooped up his cube from the desk and stuffed it into his pocket. "I wish I could scare some sense into him. Come on!"

We climbed over the cabinet and ran across the gym.

"Where's he headed?" Coach asked. "Where's the cube?"

Should I tell him? What if he really *was* a bad guy, like Jeff had said?

But Jeff had also said, "I'll wish you dead!" I pictured Coach suddenly crumpling and falling over dead. Bad guy or not, I couldn't let Jeff make that happen to him.

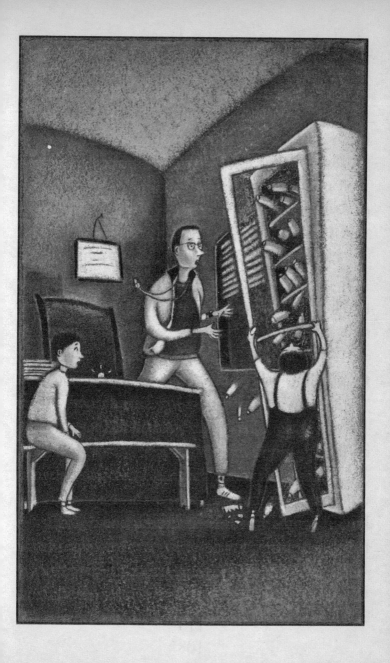

"It's home, hidden in his closet," I said, and I grabbed his sleeve. "Listen, you won't hurt him, will you?"

He put a firm hand on my shoulder the way Dad sometimes does. "Of course not. But I've got to get that cube. Come on!"

We raced out of the building. "Through the parking lot," I shouted. "It's shorter."

All of a sudden a shrill voice called my name.

"Bill Hasting? Come over here right away!"

It was Miss Bryan, the school secretary. She had her head stuck out of the window of her car and she looked upset.

"You better see what's wrong with your little brother," she said in a nervous kind of way. "I just saw him do the strangest thing."

I didn't want to stop and talk with her. Jeff could be almost halfway home by now.

"I know, Miss Bryan," I said as politely as I could. "He's trying to see how fast he can run home. Coach and I are going to . . . uh, time him."

"He's not on his way home at all," she said. "I tell you there's something wrong with that boy, running around this parking lot howling and screaming, then dashing back into the school."

"Into the school! Are you sure?"

"Certainly I'm sure! He came running out, and cut across the parking lot—I've told you children a thousand times never to do that—and then all of a sudden he stopped and started screaming. Why, I've never seen a child act so frightened."

Coach had come up behind me. "Frightened about what?" he asked.

"Well, that's what's so strange. There's nothing here that could set a child off so. He went dodging in and out between the cars as if something terrible were chasing him, and all the while he was screaming. Then he dashed back into the school—that door over there, the one by the cafeteria. I was about to go after him, but then you came by. You'd better find him and see what's wrong."

"Sure, Miss Bryan," I said. "But don't worry about Jeff. You know how he likes to kid around."

She was shaking her head as she put her car in gear. "A mighty odd kind of kidding, if you ask me."

I headed out of the parking lot but Coach stopped me.

"This way," he said. "Jeff's back in the school building."

"I know," I said, "and that's a lucky break. Now we can get home and get the cube before he does."

"No," Coach said firmly. "We have to find him, now!"

"Are you crazy? You know what wish he's going to make as soon as he gets his hands on that cube!"

"Right now that's not important. He's in trouble and we'd better find him fast."

So we ran across the parking lot to the door that led inside to the cafeteria. Coach flung open the door and I followed him in.

NINE

The cafeteria was a wreck. Chairs and tables were knocked over and plastic trays had been flung all around. Bottles of ketchup and mustard had smashed against one wall, and sticky red and yellow streaks were sliding down the tiles.

"Holy cow!" I gasped. "What happened here?"

"Can't stop to figure it out," Coach said. "We have to find Jeff."

There was no sight of him in the hall outside

the cafeteria. We ran into empty classrooms, but he wasn't there either. He wasn't in the auditorium, or the faculty room, or the music room.

And he wasn't in the sixth grade science lab, but that place looked as bad as the cafeteria. Broken glass was everywhere. Smashed test tubes and beakers were lying all over the lab benches, and chemicals were dripping onto the floor in slippery, smelly puddles.

The art room was even worse. Stools and easels had been tipped over, and paint was oozing out of broken jars and bottles. Blobs of paste splotched the walls, and the floor was a litter of broken pottery.

Coach shoved aside a pile of crayons and paintbrushes and picked something up off the floor. It was a sneaker, wet with blue paint.

"That's Jeff's!" I cried. "But I don't get it. One minute he's in a fury to get home for the cube and the next minute he's back in school throwing stuff around. How come?"

Coach looked thoughtful. "Remember what Miss Bryan told us?" he said.

"She said he started screaming, and running

around as if he were afraid."

"Right. For some reason Jeff is scared out of his senses."

Scared? Senses? The words sent my stomach rolling. I didn't know what Jeff was scared of, but all of a sudden I thought I knew why.

"Listen, Coach," I said, "when you said you wished you could scare some sense into him, did you make it a real wish? I mean with your cube?"

His face went white as he stared at me. "I must have said it just as I picked up the cube! But of course I didn't mean . . ."

A scream chopped off the rest of his words. It came from somewhere down the hall.

We raced out of the art room. "Jeff!" I shouted. "Where are you?"

There was another scream, louder and more frantic. "Get away!" Jeff shrieked. "Get away from me!"

Coach was two steps ahead of me as we rushed through the open door of the library.

Jeff was there, backed into a corner near the card catalog. He was throwing books as hard as he could at the empty room and screaming,

"Keep away! Keep away!"

As soon as he saw us he cried, "Don't let him get me! Help!"

"Who?" I shouted. "Who's after you?"

At the same time Coach yelled "Where?"

"Over there!" Jeff screamed, wagging his head in the direction of the check-out desk.

"Don't you see him? He's been ch-chasing me all over!"

"There's nobody here but Coach and me!" I shouted.

"Can't you see him? He's right over there, sneaking up on me! Oh please—help!"

In a panic he pitched another book, then

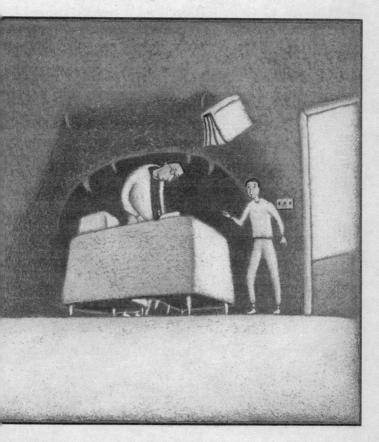

scrambled underneath the card catalog.

I ran over, crawled between the legs of the catalog, and grabbed hold of him. "Jeff, nobody's there. Honest."

He held on to me, shaking with fear and crying.

"I can see him! He *is* there!"

"Where, Jeff? For Pete's sake, *who's* there?"

"The monster! The t-toad-faced monster! He came out of the movie and now he's after me!"

"That's crazy! Things like that don't happen!"

Coach was on the floor with both of us now. He pulled Jeff out from under the card catalog and wrapped his arms around him good and tight. Jeff clung to him, sobbing and shaking. I just sat there, staring at Jeff. The whole thing was so weird I didn't know what to do.

But Coach did. He dug his cube out of his pocket and pressed it into Jeff's hand.

"Wish it away," he said. "Go on, wish the monster away."

Jeff looked at the cube a second, then closed his fist over it. He didn't say anything out loud, but I saw his lips move and I suppose he must have wished it away because pretty soon he started to calm down.

He still hung on to Coach, though. Over and over Coach kept saying, "It's okay, fella. It's all right now. The monster's gone." After a while Jeff climbed into Coach's lap and looked around to make sure. He didn't seem so terrified anymore, but he was still shaking.

"Everything's okay, Jeff," Coach said in a quiet, calm way. "There's no monster here anymore. And you know what? There never really was."

I saw Jeff go rigid again. "But I saw him! He was awful, all slimy and full of claws and he had a big ugly mouth, just like in the movie. Bill, you saw him, didn't you?"

"Only in the movie. And like I told you then, it was only make-believe."

"No! It was real! He jumped at me in the parking lot, and he ch-chased me. I tried to stop him, I threw all kinds of stuff at him, but he kept coming. It was real!"

"Listen to me, Jeff," Coach said. He sat there quietly stroking Jeff's hair and talking in that calm, soothing way, just like Dad would have done. Jeff's face was dirty and streaked with tears. Every so often he'd pull his arm across his nose and eyes, and his breath would come in little shudders of leftover sobs, but he listened carefully to every word Coach said.

"The monster was real to you, Jeff, and very, very scary. But it wasn't truly real. It was an image that came out of your own mind, a memory of something that scared you at the movies. Understand?"

Jeff shook his head no. "How c-could anything do that?" he asked in a small voice.

"I don't know, but that's what happened. And you know what? It was all my fault."

Jeff twisted around and gave Coach a puzzled look. "Your fault? How?"

"Remember when I tried to tell you and Bill how dangerous your cube could be? Remember?"

"I remember."

"Well, *my* cube was dangerous today. An accident happened with it. When you knocked over that cabinet and ran off in such a rage, I got angry too. I grabbed up my cube and started after you and I said I wished I could scare some sense into you. I didn't really mean to scare you, and I didn't plan to say that. The words just popped out because I was so angry. But because I was touching the cube—well, it happened. The scariest thing in your mind jumped out at you just as if it were real, like a nightmare coming true."

Jeff let go of Coach's cube as if it were suddenly burning his hand. It rattled onto the floor, but not one of us made a move to pick it up.

"You've had an awful time," Coach said softly. "I'm sorry for that."

Jeff squirmed in his lap. "I was going to make something awful happen to you," he said in a choked kind of voice. "I'm glad I didn't get a chance to." Then his eyes spilled over and Coach let him cry it out in quiet sobs.

I sat there, looking at the cube lying on the floor.

Finally I said, "I don't get it. How can a little chunk of metal do a weird thing like make someone imagine a monster?"

Coach hesitated. Then he said, "It's not just

a little chunk of metal. There are lots of things about these cubes that nobody understands yet. They're part of a huge experiment that went wrong. And that's why . . ."

"I know," Jeff said miserably. "That's why I have to give my cube back to you."

I was miserable too. I didn't cry, but my throat closed up and hurt something awful.

All those things I'd planned to do. I'd wanted to take all of us to the Super Bowl, and get that new mitt for Danny, and the new cars I was going to pretend Mom and Dad had won in a lottery.

None of it would happen now.

Somewhere down the hall a door slammed and we heard the whir of an electric floor sweeper. Coach and I looked at each other over Jeff's head.

"Trouble!" I said. "When the custodian sees the mess everywhere . . ."

But Coach didn't panic, not a bit. He looked at me as if he'd made up his mind about something. He smiled, and he said, "You take the cube and do a clean-up job so there won't be any mess for him to see."

"Me? With your cube?"

"Yes, Bill, I trust you. You do that while Jeff and I go to the boys' room and get *him* cleaned up. But be careful."

Careful? I picked up that cube as if it were made out of cobwebs and soap bubbles.

Coach laughed. "I didn't mean that kind of careful," he said. "What I meant was be sure to make every wish very exact."

"I get it," I said. "So it won't be like the purple sneakers ending up on a statue."

"Right! Now start with the books."

"Yeah, the books. Well, let's see . . ." I worked out my wish carefully before I put it into words. Those books had to go back on the shelves in exactly the right places.

The cube did it. Perfectly.

It took care of the art room too. I ran back there and told myself, okay, don't do anything stupid. To be safe, I started with the stools and the easels. They were easy. They jerked upright as if they'd been yanked up on invisible strings. The broken pottery went together, the crayons and paintbrushes slid back into their boxes and cans, but I had a hard time getting the paint back into the paint jars. It was tricky. First I had to wish the broken jars back together again, then I had to try not to get the colors mixed in together.

By now I was getting over being nervous. The way the paint went slurping back into the jars almost made me laugh. Some of the colors did get a little mixed, but there wasn't time to do anything about it. I grabbed Jeff's sneaker and ducked out of the art room just before Mr. Larson came around the corner with the sweeper.

He didn't see me rush into the science lab.

That job was tougher. It was easy enough to get the broken beakers and test tubes back together again, but I didn't know what to do about the spilled chemicals. I couldn't take a chance that some of them might get mixed together, like the paint. What if they blew up or something?

So I decided to leave them there, puddled all over the floor. I wished for a big sign: DANGER—SPILLED CHEMICALS. I left it taped to the door of the lab. It seemed like a cop-out, but it was the best I could do.

Besides, the cube did a nice job with the printing on the sign. DANGER was printed in red, and I hadn't even thought of that.

Now that I felt more sure of myself, the cafeteria was no problem at all.

Zing went the chairs and tables, pulled upright on their invisible strings.

Sploosh went the mustard and ketchup back into the bottles that I'd wished unsmashed. Another wish took care of the stains left on the wall.

But the trays were the most fun of all. I sent them zipping through the air like Frisbees, clattering as they piled themselves up on the counter in neat stacks. I wondered if I'd ever be able to eat lunch in that room again without remembering what they did and bursting out laughing. The other kids would think I was a nut if I told them what I was laughing about. And they wouldn't believe me, either.

At the last minute I remembered the smashed first-aid cabinet in the gym office. There wasn't time to go all the way back to the gym, so I had to take a chance on remembering everything about it. All I could do was hope that wish would work out okay.

When everything was done, I went back to find Coach and Jeff. They were waiting for me in the hall outside the boys' room.

And at the very same time along came Mr. Larson, steering the floor polisher from side to side. He nodded and smiled at us, and I smiled back, cool as can be.

"Hi, Mr. Larson," I shouted over the whir of the machine. "Got a lot of work to do today?"

"The usual," he shouted back. "All that mud you kids track in from outside every day. Well, thank goodness it's no worse than that, I always say."

"Yeah, thank goodness!" I smiled at him again as he went off down the hall.

In the front lobby we met Mr. Rose, the principal. He was locking up the office and he had his briefcase under his arm.

"Hello there," he said pleasantly. "Staying late today, boys? I bet you've been helping Coach Jackson with something."

I nodded, but Jeff hid his face by kneeling down and doing something with his sneaker laces.

"I like to stay late myself," Mr. Rose went on. "It gives me a chance to get my paperwork done while the building's quiet. Never hear a thing with the office door closed. Nice quiet afternoon today, wasn't it?"

"Yes sir," Coach agreed politely. "It certainly was. A *very* quiet afternoon." He winked at me over Jeff's head.

This time I winked back.

TEN

Jeff perked up enough to ask Coach to fly us home with his cube, but Coach smiled and said, "Sorry, fella. People would see us. Can't take a chance on that."

There wasn't any pestering from Jeff, but he looked so disappointed that Coach put an arm around his shoulder as we walked along.

Jeff was pretty quiet, but I had a whole list of questions. Like who Coach really was, and where he came from, and how come his cube had turned up in the playground. And what he had meant about "an experiment gone wrong."

His name was Mark Jackson, he told us, and he'd never been a gym teacher.

"That sure wasn't hard to figure out!" I said with a laugh. "You should've picked a better cover! But what are you? An inventor or something?"

"No, an engineer-scientist. A team of us is working at a government lab a couple hundred miles away from here."

"On teleportation?"

"It's a secret project so I can't tell you too much about it. Two weeks ago we were running our first full-scale test and something went wrong. When the teleportation machine got up to full power, the central part of it blew apart."

"Wow! Then what happened?"

"Well, a cluster of cubes, the 'brains' of the machine, scattered over hundreds of miles. We've been tracking them ever since."

All of a sudden I remembered something—the voices I'd heard when we were looking for another cube, just before Coach showed up at the playground. Those bits of talk fading in and out made sense now. The cube had tuned me in on Coach talking to one of the other scientists!

"How many cubes ended up here in Clinton?" Jeff asked.

"Only one, the one you found at the playground."

"There's something I don't understand," I said. "If the cubes blew away from the teleportation machine, how come they kept on working? Where'd they get their power from?"

"From Clinton's electric lines," Coach answered.

"Without being hitched up? Without any wires or anything? I don't get it."

"Bill, I can't tell you any more than that. The technology is top secret."

We walked a little farther without saying anything, but there was something else I just had to find out, something really important.

"The teleportation bit is neat," I said. "I've read about things like that in science fiction books. But the cube can mess around with people's thoughts, like when Jeff thought he saw the monster. Why did you build in stuff like that?"

"We didn't," Coach said slowly. "A lot of unexpected things happened, things we hadn't planned. The key directing force, you see, is mind-to-cube communication."

"You mean brain waves?"

"Something like that. Once this kind of connection was made to work, it turned out that it could work in reverse too."

"So the cube made something Jeff had been scared of jump back into his mind and seem real. Is that what happened?"

"In a way. And that's another reason why having a cube on the loose is dangerous. We just don't know what might happen. When we rebuild the machine we will have to stop that kind of feedback."

"Then it never was magic at all," Jeff said in a sad voice. "It's only teck . . . whatever that word is."

"Technology," Coach said with a smile. "Well, I don't know, Jeff. Brand-new inventions sometimes seem like magic, at first, anyway. It isn't till later, when we get everything figured out, that it isn't magic anymore, just plain old technology."

131

"It's still magic to me," Jeff said. "I don't get all that teck stuff. And besides, magic's more fun."

Mom and Dad were both in the kitchen when we got home. I introduced Coach, but I didn't say he was a scientist. He had told me not to.

"Nice to meet you," Mom said. "I didn't know the boys had a new gym teacher."

"Just for a few days," Coach said. "Mr. Willis will be back tomorrow."

Jeff and I headed for the cookie jar but Mom said, "Take it easy, boys. Don't fill up on snacks. We're having a special birthday dinner tonight."

"Yessir," Dad said proudly. "Cooked part of it myself. Just look at that fried chicken!"

"Hey, that does look great!" Coach said, and all of a sudden I got an idea.

"Mom? How about if Coach stays for dinner? He's new in Clinton and he doesn't know anybody here but us."

"Oh, I don't want to butt in on a birthday celebration. That's kind of special," Coach said.

Mom said with a smile, "We'd like very much to have you stay, Mr. Jackson."

And Dad said, "Kind of lonely in a strange town, isn't it?"

"Oh, Clinton's not so strange," Coach said, and even though it was a cornball joke everybody laughed. Except Jeff. He put the lid back on the cookie jar and went out of the kitchen with a sad, droopy sigh.

Dad shot me one of those raised eyebrow looks of his.

"Something bothering Jeff?" he asked. "He hasn't said a word. Maybe I'd better go and see what's wrong."

"No, no," I said quickly. "He's okay. Just tired, I guess. Don't worry, Coach and I will check on him."

When Coach and I got up to Jeff's room we found him sitting on the floor near the closet. He had taken the cube out of its hiding place and was holding it in his hand and looking at it sadly.

"Here it is," he said with an unhappy sigh, but he didn't make a move to hand it to Coach, or even to look at him. He kept staring at the cube with his face beginning to pucker up. I think he was trying hard not to bust out crying.

Coach squatted down beside him. After a while he sighed too, as if he had finally made up his mind about something.

"Listen, fella," he said. "How would you like to have one last wish? The three of us will go down to the playground after dinner, and if nobody's around, you can fly!"

Jeff's head jerked up. His eyes were wide and shining.

"You mean it? No kidding?"

"No kidding. You take your flight around the playground and then I take the cube back where it belongs. Okay?"

"Wow—ieeeeeeee!"

Jeff jammed the cube into his pocket and jumped up. From the sound of the thumps on the stairs he must have gone down four at a time, and he was hollering all the way.

"Hey, Mom! Dad! Isn't dinner ready yet? I can't wait!"

Mom had set the dining room table with a flower centerpiece and tall candles. "The lights have been flickering on and off all afternoon," she said. "It's really strange."

"Looks like the electric company hasn't solved its problems yet," Dad said as he lit the candles. "I wonder why there have been so many dimouts and power surges this week."

Coach gave Jeff and me a private little smile. "Whatever the reason," he said, "I have a feel-

ing it won't last too much longer."

It was a super dinner. Everything tasted so good—Dad's fried chicken, and something wonderful Mom had made out of rice and cheese, and even the vegetables. Mom and Dad and Coach got along great, and there was a lot of laughing and talking, except for Jeff. He tore into his food in a hurry and didn't pay much attention to any of the talk. Every so often, though, he'd look over at Coach and flap his elbows like a bird.

Finally Mom brought in a big birthday cake and we all sang "Happy Birthday" to Dad. Jeff was in such a rush he didn't even ask for a second piece. He slid off his chair so fast it almost tipped over, and said to Coach, "Okay, let's go!"

"Slow down, honey," Mom said. "It's birthday present time." She gave Dad a beautiful scarf she'd woven for him, all soft and warm, with a design of wonderful colors. Dad loved it.

"Exactly the thing to wear on a balmy May evening like this," he said as he wound it around his neck.

We all laughed and then I said, "Jeff and I

have a present for you too. I'll get it."

"*I* will!" Jeff yelled. "I'm faster!" He rushed out of the room and took the stairs two at a time.

Dad watched him with a smile. "Is that the boy who came drooping home from school today too tired to talk?" he asked.

"He's anxious to get down to the playground," Coach said smoothly. "I promised he could show me something after dinner."

Jeff came skidding back into the dining room and thrust our package at Dad. "Here!" he gasped. "Happy birthday from me and Bill— and it didn't mess up anything anyplace!"

I could have kicked him. Dad looked puzzled, but as he unwrapped the package and caught sight of the rock he forgot about what Jeff had said.

"A desert rose! And what a beauty! This is a great specimen, boys. Where in the world did you find it? The rock shop at the mall?"

"No," Jeff said proudly. "It came straight from—"

"Let's clear the table, Jeff!" I cut in quickly. "Right now!

"You mushbrain!" I hissed at him in the kitchen. "You want to blow the whole thing?"

As we were shoving some plates into the dishwasher, Mom came in with a handful of coffee cups. "Okay, clean-up squad," she said, "Dad and I will finish here. You run along to the playground."

So after Coach's good-byes and handshakes and thank-yous to Mom and Dad, we were on our way to the playground at last.

"You guys walk too slow," Jeff complained. "I'll meet you there."

He started to run ahead, but Coach grabbed him.

"No," Coach said firmly. "We all stay together."

Jeff grumbled, but Coach wouldn't let him go ahead of us. There was a nothing's-going-to-stop-me-from-flying-this-time look on Jeff's face.

And the cube was in his pocket.

ELEVEN

We hadn't gone much more than a block before we saw that the whole neighborhood was swarming with electric company crews. Trucks filled with equipment were all over the place, and men high up in cherry pickers were working on the overhead wires.

"Wonder what's going on," I said.

"We'd better find out," Coach said.

Jeff tugged away. "Aw come on," he complained. "It'll start getting dark soon."

"Hold on," Coach insisted. "This could be something important."

So Jeff stood by, grumpily scuffing the sidewalk, while Coach talked with the foreman.

"We're installing current-overload sensors and automatic cut-off switches in this area," the man said.

"You are?" Coach sounded startled.

"Yeah, there's been so much demand for current around here lately, the company's afraid of a power failure that would black out the whole town."

I could see a troubled look on Coach's face. "How long before you go operational?" he asked.

"Not long. Ten minutes, maybe less. This is the last sector to go on-line."

Coach came back over to us. "Jeff," he said quietly, "I'm sorry, fella, really sorry, but I'm afraid you're not going to fly after all."

"What do you mean?" Jeff yelled.

"Look, it's complicated, but what it adds up to is that in a few minutes the cube won't work."

140

"WON'T WORK? Sure it will. It always works!"

"Jeff, listen. I can't let you fly now. It's too dangerous."

"But you promised!" Jeff shouted. "I *will* do it, I *will*!" He whirled away from us and was around the corner before I knew what was happening.

Coach turned pale. Then he took off after Jeff. I caught up with him at the corner, but Jeff was nowhere in sight.

"Quick, which way would he go?" Coach cried.

"I don't know, maybe the shortcut through Mr. Miller's yard. Follow me."

Why are we always chasing after Jeff? I thought angrily as I ran. It seems I've spent most of this whole day running after him. What's the big deal this time?

Then it hit me like a fist in the stomach, and I ran as fast as I could. All that stuff the electric company men were installing would be ready to be turned on any minute now. And if Jeff were up in the air when those sensors and switches went into action, the current the cube was pulling from the power lines would suddenly be cut off. Jeff would come crashing down. He could be hurt, even killed.

Coach and I dashed past the trees at the edge of the playground, but it was too late. Jeff was already flying, whooshing smoothly upward like a transcontinental jet. Up he soared with perfect control. I realized that he must have spent a lot of time thinking about flying and planning exactly how to do it. If I hadn't been so scared, it would have been fun to watch him.

But I *was* scared. So was Coach.

"How'll we get him down?" I yelled. "How long before they turn all that stuff on?"

"Not long enough," Coach shouted back. Then he pulled his own cube out of his pocket and almost before I knew it he was in the air too, chasing Jeff high above the ground!

It was getting dark now. Lights were coming on in the houses near the playground, and the streetlights turned on too. Ten minutes, the foreman had said. Ten minutes or less. How much time was left? I wondered frantically.

Coach went streaking up close to Jeff and

made a grab for his foot. He missed, and shot past him.

Jeff thought it was a game of tag.

"Can't catch me!" he yelled, and I felt the wind whip over my head as he swooped down and up again, whizzing out of Coach's reach.

"Jeff!" I shouted over the tight fear in my throat. "It isn't a game! Come down! You'll get hurt!"

"Wheeeeeeeeeeeee! This is the greatest!" he shouted back. "Hey, Coach, can you do this?" He pulled his legs up to his chest and shot them out again, looping and twirling in such a wild rush of motion that it made me dizzy to watch him. In the twilight I couldn't see Coach's face clearly, and he was flying too fast anyhow, but I could feel the fear we both shared.

Jeff came shooting past me again. "Jeff!" I yelled. "Come down!"

He just laughed, and off he went, soaring up even higher. Coach was close behind him, but even though he had a long reach he couldn't grab hold of Jeff. Every time he made a grab, Jeff would tuck his arms and legs tight against his body and shoot up out of the way.

And each one of those thrusts and twists took them both even higher.

Coach flicked out his hand again, and this time he managed to touch one of Jeff's sneakers. I held my breath, hoping he'd be able to get a firm hold on Jeff's foot and pull him down. He couldn't.

And then I heard Coach shout, "Tag! You're It!"

Had he gone nuts? Any minute now the electric company men would finish installing the new equipment and turn it on. And then both Coach and Jeff would come crashing down. They'd both be piles of broken bones on the ground.

"Come down! Stop! Come down!" I shrieked, but my voice was flung right back at me by the whistling, swooshing sound of the two of them flying through the air above me.

Jeff was diving after Coach now, laughing and whooping as he plunged downward.

Downward? All of a sudden I realized what Coach was doing!

He wasn't playing at all. He had tricked Jeff. All the while Jeff was chasing him Coach was bringing them both closer to the ground.

They must have been about thirty feet off the ground when Coach finally let Jeff close in on him.

"I'll get you now!" Jeff shouted.

But Coach twisted around, made a lunge for Jeff, and locked an arm around his waist.

"No fair!" Jeff yelled. "*I'm* the one who's It!"

I could see Coach hanging on to Jeff hard. They were heading down in a big slanting circle. If only Coach could ease them both down for a landing before it was too late.

All at once everything went black. The streetlights went off. The lights in the houses went off.

And in the dark I heard a whumping kind of sound. It was the sound of Coach and Jeff hitting the ground.

It was so dark I couldn't see where they had fallen.

"Where are you?" I shouted frantically. "Are you okay? Tell me you're okay, please, TELL ME!"

There wasn't a sound.

A few seconds later the lights came back on, and I could see them sprawled on the ground not far away.

I ran over, but I was almost afraid to look.

I didn't see any blood, but they were both so still. Then Jeff's arm moved, and Coach gave a faint groan. They'd both had the breath knocked out of them, but they were alive!

Jeff got his wind back first. He scrambled to his feet and tugged at Coach.

"That was great!" he said excitedly. "Come on, let's do it again!"

Coach sat up slowly. He had bruises, but no broken bones. Mostly he was just stunned. He sat there on the ground with his knees pulled up to his chin and his head bent down, trying to get back his breath.

"Come on!" Jeff begged again. "Let's get a running start and do it some more! Only this time watch the landing, will you?"

Coach lifted his head. If it had been me, I think I would have smacked Jeff, hard. But Coach didn't. He just spoke very quietly, and very slowly.

"We are not going to do it again," he said.

Jeff seemed surprised. "How come?" he asked.

"The cube, please." Coach held out his hand, palm up.

"Aw, rats," Jeff grumbled. "Just because of one bad landing? Come on, be a good sport."

"JEFF!" I yelled. Now that I knew he wasn't dead or even hurt, I was furious. "You little jerk! Don't you know how close you came to getting killed? And Coach too, all because of you!"

"You're nuts." He laughed. "I've got this flying thing all figured out." He turned to Coach and said, "And the cube worked just fine. How come you said it wouldn't work?"

In the glow of the streetlight I could see an awful lot of feelings mixed together in Coach's face: anger, laughter, and a kind of wonder. All he said, though, was "The cube, Jeff." And again his hand was out, waiting.

I wasn't sure whether Jeff would give in or not.

I was ready to clobber him if he didn't.

He did, but in his own way. "Aw . . . okay. Catch!"

With a flick of his thumb he flipped the cube straight up into the air. It spun for a second, flashing soft and silvery. On its downward swing Coach caught it with a sweep of his hand.

"Let's go," he said. "I'll walk you boys home."

The streets were quiet now. The electric company crews had driven away, and there was no one around.

I wasn't mad at Jeff anymore. A kind of sadness had crowded out my anger. In a little while Coach and the cube would both be gone, and I knew I'd miss them both.

When we stopped in front of our house Coach looked at Jeff and me seriously.

"Listen, boys," he said, "you mustn't say a word to anyone about the cube, or about any of the things that happened while you had it. I know it'll be tough not telling your friends or your mom and dad, but it has to be a secret. Understand?"

"Sure," Jeff said. "Who'd ever believe us anyway!"

"Don't worry," I added, "it'll stay a secret.

150

And, Coach? I want to tell you . . . well, you're an okay guy. Thanks for . . ."

Thanks for saving Jeff's life was what I wanted to say, but it didn't come out that way.

"Thanks for going after this little pest," I said.

Coach knew what I meant. He nodded, and punched me lightly on the arm. He ruffled Jeff's hair, then smiled at us both and walked quickly away.

Jeff and I sat on the front steps for a long time, talking about a lot of things.

"It was fun having the cube, wasn't it?" Jeff said with a sigh.

"Yeah," I said. "But some of the things that happened weren't fun at all."

"I know," Jeff admitted. "But I don't want to forget any of it, ever. Not even the scary and bad parts."

"Me too."

We each did our own thinking for a while. Then Jeff said, "I feel different tonight."

"So do I, more tired than I've ever been in my whole life."

"No, I mean a different kind of different."
He stopped, looking uncertain. "I feel . . . well,
I'm sorry for all the dumb things I did, Bill. I'm
sorry for the way I acted sometimes."

I couldn't believe my ears! It was the first
time I'd ever heard him talk that way.

"It's okay," I said awkwardly.

"But you know what I'm sorry for most of
all?" His grin came back again. "Most of all I'm
sorry it's all over!"

I laughed. "I bet it isn't all over," I said.
"Soon as Coach and his team get the teleportation machine working right, all kinds of things
are going to happen."

"To us?"

"No. They'll be big things, really important
things."

"Like what?"

"I don't know for sure. Maybe Coach's machine will be used to clean up after earthquakes,
or rescue people, or get sunken treasure out of
the ocean where it's too deep for divers to go.

"Could the machine do all that?" Jeff asked.

"Sure. Think about all the things one little
cube did! I guess from now on, whenever

there's a news story about something really unusual, I'm going to be wondering if Coach and the machine had something to do with it." I leaned back against the top step. "Gee," I said, "wouldn't it be great to be a news reporter and be in on all that stuff. Maybe when I grow up I'll—"

"Not me!" Jeff broke in. "I'm going to be a scientist like Coach!"

He jumped up, full of excitement again. "You can report on things, but I'm going to make them happen! And maybe I won't even wait till I'm grown-up!"

"What are you talking about?" I said.

"Listen, Bill, if I start learning about that teck stuff now, I might be able to make my own cube!"

"Don't be nuts," I said. "A kid couldn't do that."

"Yeah? Well, I'm gonna find a way to get some magic again, you just watch!"

I'll watch, all right. When you've got a kid brother like him, anything can happen!